KNIGHT PACK BOOK 2

Elissa Daye

World Castle Publishing, LLC
Pensacola, Florida
Copyright © Elissa Daye 2019
Paperback ISBN: 9781950890224
eBook ISBN: 9781950890231
First Edition World Castle Publishing, LLC, September 9, 2019
http://www.worldcastlepublishing.com

Licensing Notes

Cover: Melissa Davis
Editor: Maxine Bringenberg

Chapter 1

"*Move*," the voice ordered.

It almost always started out that way, a simple haunting voice. Lila shivered slightly as she turned on her electronic voice phenomenon (EVP) recorder and started her questions.

"Did you just tell me to move?" A cold blast of air went to her back and she knew she was not going to get anything on EVP, but Lila left it on regardless. Why would they talk to a piece of equipment when it was so much easier to just talk to her? That was something Lila never quite understood. As a medium, she provided easier access for the spirits who crept through the shadows.

"What do you want?" More chills.

"*Help me*," came the whisper of a younger voice.

Lila turned around, trying to see the body behind the voice, but there was no one there. She should be used to this by now. They were always following her. Her life had been filled with disembodied voices, blurry shapes, and dark shadows. At twenty-five Lila had plenty of experience with them.

Sometimes they were so loud, Lila had to focus on shutting down the lines of connection, not to mention shielding herself from their overpowering energies. At times Lila found herself bargaining out loud with them; Let me sleep and I'll help you in the morning. Unfortunately, most spirits had no sense of time. Death was timeless for those on an infinite loop on the other side.

"*Get out!*" It was the first voice again. Definitely male, and very aggressive toward intruders.

"Damn it!" Lila did not want to wait for her team to back her up, but she had little choice in the matter. When they were involved in a joint investigation, Lila had less control over the situation than she did when she was flying solo. Since their mission tonight was to capture as much proof as possible of something paranormal, she couldn't just work her magic on the situation.

The Templar Paranormal Research Association (TPRA) was waiting outside while Lila did a psychic sweep of the house. Unlike many paranormal investigation groups, this team believed that mediums were very helpful in detecting spirit activity. Good thing, because Lila had gotten tired of going the solo road for so long. She was what one might consider a closet medium, who was also a closet witch, hiding everything about herself from the outside world. It was just easier that way.

A chair toppled over near her, and the air around her turned freezing cold. She heard him whisper beside her ear. "*Leave.*"

"I'm not afraid of you."

Lila switched on her flashlight and moved it across the

room. She did not see any shapes or shadows, but the air was crackling around her. This was not your everyday entity. He was much darker, and definitely had a problem with women.

"Get out!"

"No." The front door opened, and while Lila expected one of her teammates to enter, there was no one there. "Is that the best you got?"

The door slammed shut and the locked turned in place. Four more loud bangs erupted around her as other doors in the house started to close. The windows nearby started to rattle as if the winds were pushing hard against them from the outside.

Lila could hear John outside. "You okay in there?"

"Yes. We're just getting started in here, John." Lila went to the door and turned the lock. She tried to open the door, but it would not budge. Walking to the windows, Lila unlocked one and attempted to raise it. No luck. This was a first.

"Open the door," Lila ordered the ghost. When she heard the sound of clopping footsteps above her, Lila watched for any sign of the creeper. The sound echoed down the hallway, then made its way to the top of the stairs.

"You should have left." The younger voice was quivering behind her. *"He's going to get you now."*

Lila grabbed the doorknob and tried to yank the door open. She wasn't exactly a lightweight, so opening it should not have been so difficult. While she could use some of her magic, she had promised herself not to reveal every inch of herself to the investigators. Some things were better left hidden. Lila clicked on her walkie. "John, push on the door. I may be in some trouble here."

John and Lila worked on opening the door for what seemed like an eternity, and all the while the footsteps were moving closer down the stairs. The room was getting hot and the furnace hadn't even kicked on. It only got hot when they were very angry. This was no ordinary entity.

"I'll go. I promise. Just open the door."

Was that her voice shaking? Lila seriously needed to keep calm. Half of the problem with fear was that she needed to control the thoughts feeding it. Lila kept telling herself that there was nothing this entity could do to hurt her. She ran that thought through her mind over and over, but the slash of red-hot fire on her back reminded her that yes, it could. From the corner of her eye she saw books floating off the shelf before they were launched at her. She ducked, but not fast enough to avoid all of them. Two of them pelted her in the head.

"John, get me out of here now!"

John was finally able to open the window. "Lila, come on. Hurry!" He yelled out to her.

As Lila climbed through the window, it did not escape her attention that sharp knives were now levitating through the kitchen and were starting to pick up speed through the air. She barely made it out the window before the knives collided into the door where she had been standing. Lila leapt from the porch and almost collapsed on the grass. She tried to slow her breathing, as every breath seemed to come in sharp gasps.

"You all right, Lila?" John asked her. The thirty-year-old investigator was the founder of the TPRA, and had seen his fair share of hauntings, but even he seemed to be in shock.

"I'm fine." She was only half convinced herself.

"What was that thing?"

"If I'd had more time I could tell you more. My first impression is a demonic entity. He definitely did not want us in the house. There was also a child's voice." Lila sighed. "Which isn't something you can trust, really. Sometimes children's voices are actually demons in disguise. A lot of people fall for it, because they seem so innocent."

"Is it safe to go back in?"

"No. I think you should call it, John. I'm not going back in there. I wouldn't expect anyone else to go in there either. That thing is angry."

John looked disappointed. "That's too bad. We've been waiting over a year to get into that place."

"Well, if you really want to head back in, I'll be waiting outside at command. Maybe it's just me he was irritated with. Sometimes that happens."

"I think we'll check in with the others."

The two of them went to the tent that had been set up out front. Lila knew the answer before it even came. There was nothing that kept these guys from investigating. If they went, though, it would be at their own peril. Lila wasn't even sure she could cleanse the house without more help. She was good, but this thing was nasty.

Lila listened to John explain the situation, and waited for her moment to interrupt them. She did not need to, though. At that moment a loud explosion erupted from inside the house.

"What the...?" Daniel shook his head. "Dude, I don't think I want to go in there."

Lila held the back of her shirt up. "It's vicious."

"Holy crap. You're bleeding, Lila. That looks pretty deep." James touched her skin gingerly and Lila winced.

"Yeah, he's too much for me to take on by myself, and apparently he is still angry."

John sighed. "I think we have to call it."

"Hey, there will be other places," Daniel assured him. "Besides, no hunt is worth getting hurt."

"True. We need to get you checked out, Lila." John found the first aid kit. "Let's get it cleaned up and see if you need some medical attention."

Lila stood there and tried to not grind her teeth as John cleaned up the scratches on her back. They burned like hellfire—that thing was sadistic. Thankfully, the people who had moved into the house had been smart enough to move their kids out as soon as possible.

"I've put a few bandages over it. I don't think you're going to need stitches, but it's not like any scratch I've ever seen.

"Agreed," Lila sighed. "Most of them usually disappear. Did you get a picture of it?"

"Yep. All right, everyone. Let's pack it up and get out of here."

They spent the next hour getting everything put back in the van. When they were finally ready to take off, Lila looked through the window and saw a shadowed figure staring at them from the window. She sensed its eyes on her, and shivered slightly as she got into the van.

"So, where are we going next week?"

Lila punched John on the shoulder. She had barely made it out this time, and he was already thinking about where they would go next. Lila would have kicked him had he not been driving. He was right though. They all lived for these moments, no matter how frightening they could be.

As they drove away, Lila heard a voice whisper to her. *"He's coming for you."*

Lila shuddered. This wasn't the first time a spirit had followed her. It probably wouldn't be the last, either. That was the way it worked sometimes. She was still not quite sure what she had done to attract his attention. Engaging the child? Maybe the child was a spirit under its control. Sometimes demonic entities liked to collect other spirits to manipulate and torture.

"You're awfully quiet, Lila," Daniel called up to her.

"I'm just trying to take it in," she lied. That wasn't it at all. She was gearing up for war. This thing had marked her, and in doing so gave her his intent. That must mean it was her job to take him out. They often lashed out at those that had the ability to break their link on this earth. She would deal with it eventually, but not when these guys were around her. Lila did not want to put them in danger.

As they continued down the road, Lila pressed play on her EVP.

"Get out...."

"Whoa! I heard that." John was visibly impressed. "That's one gravelly voice."

"At least we got something," Daniel interjected. "I also got a picture of the shadow in the window."

"You saw it too?" Lila asked him in surprise. Sometimes the men couldn't see the shapes she did. She never knew what was visible to them and what wasn't.

"Yes. Look." Daniel handed her the digital camera.

"Wow...so dark even in daylight. That's just crazy." And

powerful, she thought to herself. Most entities waited until the nighttime to show themselves. This thing had no trouble gathering what he wanted and manipulating the energy around him. Lila felt the need to research everything she could about this house. There was still a lot to do.

She handed the camera back to Daniel and closed her eyes as she tried to do a mental block. Lila could feel the darkness surrounding her. When she got home, she was going to have to do a full aura cleansing. While the men continued to talk, she blocked them out and focused on what she needed for that moment in time. She had a feeling that she was about to be sent down a large rabbit hole, chasing after something that was much bigger than herself.

Chapter 2

Lila was still a little shaken by the time she made it back to the small house that she called her own. That had been one of the closest calls she'd ever experienced. She was still trying to figure out what had happened. One second she was just looking through the old house, the next she was being attacked by something demonic.

Looking in the mirror, she winced when she saw the deep red gashes on her back. That was going to be hard to clean. She didn't think that the wound was deep enough to be concerned with, though. It just hurt like hell any time her shirt slid over it. Good thing her bra didn't touch it. Not that she needed an excuse not to wear one. Half of the time she flung it off the second she walked into her house.

Lila glanced around at the small house, the one her grandmother had left her when she passed. She touched the kitchen counter, still the ugly pea green that it had been for the last seventy years. Lila was loathe to change it—not that her job paid her enough to do much anyway. She wasn't

11

complaining — she made enough to live off of as a part time editor for a publishing house — but if she had to support more than herself that pay would not be enough. At least she was putting her bachelor's degree to good use, unlike many postgraduates.

College. Lila shuddered. It had not been the best experience for her. Surrounded by roommates who had been more interested in partying than actually cracking a book, Lila had found herself isolated in her room most of the time. She found it hard to deal with people sometimes. The only peace she had found was through the pagan student association, which she had attended on a whim after finding herself disillusioned with the religion her family had forced on her all her life. Lila had come to feel that religion should be a choice, something that resonated its truth inside you, not one you had to do just to make your family happy.

Of course, choosing this path had cost her the only family she had left. Grandma Tilly, her paternal grandmother, had taken her in when her parents had kicked her out. That was when she learned her grandmother had a few secrets of her own. Tilly had been a solitary practitioner herself, and shared her time as a witch with Lila. Not long after opening herself up to her true path, Lila had started to understand why she had always felt like she was being watched her entire childhood. She felt that way even now, but there was a reason for that. Spirits were attracted to her because Lila was a natural born medium, just like Grandma Tilly.

Lila sighed. It had only been six months since Grandma Tilly had passed. She missed her dreadfully. From time to time, Lila felt her loving glow and smelled the rose perfume she used to put on every morning. While it brought her a little peace, she was still reminded how empty her life had become. At twenty-five, Lila had very little left in the world, except the pursuit of the one thing Tilly and her had shared. It made her feel closer to her even though she was far away in the spirit realm. "Oh, Tilly. What have I done? That thing was nasty."

Careful, child.

Lila smiled as the sweet smell of roses wafted toward her. "I miss you, Tilly."

All is well.

Lila felt like the spirit wrapped her in a warm hug, and a tear fell down her face. This life was a lonely life, but she just didn't have the social skills that others did. Making friends had always been hard, especially if she had to hide who she was. Acquaintances, those were far easier—like the TPRA. While she spent a lot of time with them, the only thing they ever talked about was the houses they were hunting. There was an easy friendship between them, but nothing that extended past their hunts.

Lila walked over to the mirror and looked inside. She didn't see anything special to look at—brown eyes, long brown hair, and a pinched nose. A splatter of freckles, which she'd had since she was a child, crossed her nose and cheeks.

Her childhood. Back then she'd still had her siblings to play with. They had been close once, but that had all changed the minute she had been forced out of the family. Blinking, she pushed that out of her head. "Stop that, Lila. You know it doesn't help to dwell."

Besides, she had a book to edit. Thankfully, it was an easy read—a murder mystery. One of her favorite authors to work with, too. She walked over to her desk and pulled out her laptop. She spent the next couple of hours finishing up the last two chapters so that she could send it back to the author to approve the changes. When she was done she rubbed her temples and yawned.

As Lila got up from her chair, she saw a dark shadow standing outside of her window. "Damn it."

Something had followed her home. It wasn't the first time that Lila had that happen. She really needed to be much more careful when she was out on a hunt. Lila would have to work on her shield. If she had covered her energy trail, it would not have been able to follow her home.

Lila refused to show fear. Opening her front door, she stepped outside. The shadowed figure moved further down the outside wall of her house. While it wasn't welcome here, it was not the exact same energy she had encountered at the house.

"What are you doing here?"

"Warning."

Warning? About what? And who was this thing. "Who are you?"

Ben.

"Benjamin Vinson?" Lila asked warily.

"Trapped."

Lila knew there was still a lot that she did not know about the Vinson house. The people who had let them investigate it were the new owners. There had been a fair amount of activity there over the decades. Benjamin Vinson was the first owner, the man who had the house built in the early 1800s. The Vinsons had been the owners from one generation to the next, until the last of the line had passed away, leaving the estate up for auction. The new owners had bought the house to flip it for a profit. The minute they had started to make any kind of changes, they had come face to face with one problem after another.

Lila glanced at the shadow, whose dark shape was only broken by the white light where the eyes glowed hauntingly. She sensed there was truth to what the spirit said, but there was a darkness that made her wary. It was a trick.

"Go away."

The shadow rushed at her, fading just before it reached her. She shook in the air of its aftermath. Were they all trapped there by that thing? It was possible. What she felt had been demonic, for sure. Any demonic entity had the ability to possess others to the point of their own self-destruction, and if they passed away while under its control, they were destined to an eternity enslaved on the other side. Lila would not wish that on any soul.

Did that mean she was going to help them? Lila sighed. How could she refuse? To do so would go against her own personal covenant. Harm none. Which meant she was in whether she wanted to be or not. She only hoped that she would still be standing at the end of it all. That thing was not something she really wanted to deal with.

Lila went back inside and realized it was three in the morning. She needed to get some sleep. Tomorrow, she would have to tackle another editing job so that she could pay her bills. Changing into her nightgown, Lila pulled the covers back and slid beneath the cool sheets. Maybe if she were lucky she wouldn't have the same dream she had every night. Closing her eyes, she waited for sleep to take her.

In a matter of moments she was transported to another time and place, running through the forest from the eyes that followed her. Golden eyes — or were they blue? Every time she looked over her shoulder they were the same. Her legs ran as fast as they could carry her.

As the dark shadows tried to envelope her, a snarling growl intercepted them. His eyes were blue, but flashed golden as the rage took over. Ripping into each thing in his path, he tore them into tattered shreds. The wolf turned to face her, yet did not come any closer. His eyes were tearing into her very soul.

Lila stood there shaking, afraid of him, but not for the reason other people might have been. She knew what was going to happen next. It always happened. The wolf contorted and twisted before her, turning into something else altogether. In his place was an attractive man, with the same piercing blue eyes. His blond hair, golden skin, and devilish grin was far more dangerous than anything else she'd ever seen in her life.

He stepped closer, and for every step he took, she moved further back from him. This man, he wanted something she had never given anyone, and if she gave in to it, he would consume every inch of her. And yet, somewhere inside her, Lila wanted to know how that would feel.

Tonight, the dream was different. She stood her ground and let him take her into his arms. His mouth came down to hers as he pulled her roughly against his body. As his lips plundered hers, her heart started to beat in her throat. His hands slid behind her head and pulled it back as he layered kisses across her face and down her neck. She was having trouble breathing as his heat filtered into her body.

"I want you, Lila."

In her dream state, Lila managed to regain control. She shoved him away from her and held her hands up. "I can't."

Lila started to run from him again — not afraid of him, but afraid of what could happen if she gave in to the feelings that were racing through her. She did not understand the way his touch affected her. Lila craved more, but she wasn't sure what it was she wanted. While she had read plenty on the subject, she had no experience with it, and even in her dream state she was embarrassed by it. She would only end up disappointing him.

The wolf followed her, unwilling to give up on the chase. He wanted her, she knew it, but Lila could not give in. The wolf arced through the air and pushed her to the ground. They rolled several times, and when they stopped, Lila found herself pinned, not by the wolf, but the man who could seduce the angels from the heavens.

She tried to push him off, but he captured her hands with his own. He pushed them back to the ground as his mouth ravaged hers. A heat coiled somewhere deep inside of her, and she was soon whimpering beneath him, wanting things she could not quite understand. Her need for him grew to a fiery pitch as his mouth worked its magic over hers. When he released her hands, she wrapped them around his head and sighed against him.

His hands worked her shirt over her stomach and caressed it gently as he pulled it over her head. His mouth ran a path of hot kisses down her face, her neck, all the way to the space between her breasts, where its hot breath seemed so mar her skin moments before he devoured it with his mouth. Lila arched into his touch, ready for more, but as the dream started to get interesting, he seemed to fade from sight as a loud beeping sound permeated the air. Lila tried to call him back, but everything around her disappeared and the sound only continued.

As Lila woke up, she rolled over and groaned. Smashing her hand down on her alarm, she then brought her knees to her chest, realizing that the deep longing was still emanating through her body. A need inside her roared its ugly head, but Lila had no idea how to quench it. She hugged a pillow tight and tried to calm herself. Looking over at her alarm she wanted to toss it out the window, because for the first time in her life she actually felt almost alive. It was a shame that a dream lover was the only one to make her feel that way.

She sighed aloud and threw the covers off her body. Whether she wanted to or not, the day was starting. Lila still had quite a bit of work to do today. No time like the present.

Chapter 3

It was now the witching hour, the time where it was said that spirits walked the earth. Lila was holed up in another attic with her EVP recorder and walkie so she could contact the team if she needed them. Except for the TPRA, the house was empty, the lights were out, and the air was still.

"You all right up there, Lila?"

"I told you I'm okay, John. You can stop asking now. I'll let you know if I need you, promise."

It was clear that John was still feeling a tad bit guilty about sending her in solo at the last house. That was the most wicked experience of her life. She was still reeling from it.

During the week, she had started reaching out to anyone in the area that had dealt with the Vinson house. Very little was known. The Vinsons had all died relatively young, well before their time. Most were sudden deaths—heart attacks, strokes, and embolisms seemed to be at the top of the list. Could the demonic entity be responsible for these events? It was possible, but no one could really know for sure. While she had thought that all the living members of the house were dead, Lila was surprised to find one of the females had survived, probably because she had left the family far behind.

Lila had tried to find that woman's descendants, but she was having trouble finding any specific information. The last place the woman had been seen was near Rainier, which was three hours south of here, and close to a place that Lila was afraid to visit. Witch's Hollow. She shivered. Lila did not want to go there, not if she could help it. From what she knew of the area, the ley lines were so radical the earth around them seemed to shift. Not to mention the fact that she hadn't been around a whole population of witches before.

Her beliefs she rarely shared with anyone else, because being a solitary practitioner was far safer than letting anyone in. She had done that once, and lost everyone she'd ever loved, all because she could no longer relate to the religion that seemed to saturate every inch of her family. Lila had not found peace anywhere else. It really was as simple as that, but apparently that was too hard for other people to understand. That was life, unfortunately.

At least Grandma Tilly had understood that. She couldn't help wondering what Tilly would have done in this situation. Would she try to find more information about Virginia Vinson? Or would she drop it? Tilly hadn't been one to chase the spirits the way that Lila was. It was just what she wanted to do. She was thankful that her job allowed her to do just that. As an editor, she could work anywhere in the world. So, Lila spent her time hunting where she could and helping families who needed help crossing over spirits that were meddling in their houses. She wasn't well known in the field, as Lila only helped a handful of people here and there. Her name was known only through word of mouth, and her services were always free.

While Lila had spent time researching the Vinson house, she was also trying to dull the aftereffects of the entity. Saging her aura had only worked for the first few hours after her first exposure. After Benjamin Vinson, she started to feel the same dark energy from the house circling around her own. The being was desperate to gain entrance, but Lila had every inch of her tiny house protected. She had never seen a spirit use so much of the energy around her to manipulate actual objects the way it had. This was something else entirely. Something that could very well be the reason that so many people had died. Lila was not going to be the next on its list.

While it had been a scary encounter, Lila knew she would not rest until she knew what was happening there. If she could help release the spirits that were trapped there, she would do everything she could to make it happen. She would not stop until she did.

After the incidents at the Vinson house, the TPRA had decided to institute a new rule that Lila was not allowed to go into the houses by herself. Lila appreciated their support, but sometimes it was easier to be alone without any other human distractions. For now, she was going along with them as best she could. Right now they were working in teams; however, the attic was not big enough for more than one person, so Lila had asked to come up first. John was sitting on the floor downstairs, waiting to switch places with her.

"Is anyone up here?" The lights on the K2 meter bounced from green to yellow. It was clear that there was something there. Lila crept as quietly as she could through the chaos of boxes in the attic. She stood up as far as she could without bumping her head, and looked up at the rafters in the ceiling. Lila could see a few dusty webs hanging down, and started to chuckle to herself.

"What's so funny up there?"

"Nothing." Lila knew how afraid John was when it came to spiders. It was a good thing John had stayed down below; he was such a ninny. If there was any spider perched in one of those webs, he would have run screaming like a little girl down the stairs. While that would have made for an amazing laugh, it would definitely have interrupted their investigation.

"What are you hiding?"

"Just some spider webs, relax. I'm going to knock some of them down."

"Be careful," he warned her.

Lila rolled her eyes. See, ninny. A few little webs weren't going to hurt anyone. Before Lila started to knock down the webs, she placed the K2 meter on the box below, making sure it was secure. Picking up a hanger that was laying on the floor, she started to pull the strands down from the ceiling. No spiders came toppling down on her, but she was half tempted to tell John they had. Sometimes he deserved the grief they gave him; plus, he dished it out well enough for all of them.

Now that the webs would not be a distraction to their *fearless* leader, Lila picked up the K2 meter to see if she could get a better sense of where the energy was coming from. Closing her eyes, she put her hand to her head to help clear her thoughts. Sometimes these electronic gadgets really only took her so far in an investigation. While they were handy to those without extra sensory perception, they sometimes made making a spiritual contact difficult. The bars on the K2 were stagnant. No more movement.

"I guess I'll have to do this the hard way." Lila put down the EVP recorder and the K2 monitor and sat on the floor. She breathed in the air around her and waited for the spirits to settle in. Opening her eyes, Lila mentally gathered every ounce of determination. The air around her shifted. A cold air started to send clouds of cold vapor on her cheeks. Lila knew someone was there.

"Where are you?" She did not have to wait long for an answer.

"*Here.*"

Lila turned to the sound of the voice. "Why are you still here? Who are you?"

"*Sam.*"

"Your name is Sam?" Lila closed her eyes and tried to take the pictures that were being sent to her mind. Lila switched on her EVP recorder. "This is a recorder. Can you speak into it?"

Lila waited to see if there would be any more from the spirit. The K2 started to light up, so Lila asked a few more questions. "What is your name? Do you know where you are? How did you die? Did you live here?"

"*Sam,*" the voice whispered to her again. "*He's coming for you.*"

Lila shivered and turned off the EVP recorder. She wasn't sure she wanted the others to hear a warning for her. They wouldn't understand it, but she did. Lila had been very careful in how she dealt with the spirit realm over the past few weeks. However that entity identified itself, it was clear that it had nothing better to do. Like most dark beings, if it felt a threat it was in defense mode. Those kind of things were much happier to be hidden from the world. Any time someone broadcasted their existence, they were in attack mode. Exposure was seen as a threat.

Lila could not let that stop her if she were going to keep it from herding other spirits under its control. She only had one choice — head to the one place she was afraid to visit. Witch's Hollow. Lila would only do that if nothing else panned out. One step at a time. A box shook near her, but she ignored it. With John safe below, she took a chance and cast a spell of protection around her. White light gathered in a ball inside her. It grew and grew until every inch of her was surrounded in its protective glow.

She whispered, "*I am safe, I am loved, I am protected. You are not welcome here.*"

The box shook again and a frisson of electricity seemed to crackle around her. Lila opened her hands and sent a burst of light into the room, erasing all the shadows that crept nearby. She knew it was only a short fix, but it was certainly better than nothing at this point. Something would have to be done soon.

"Everything okay up there?" John called up. He must have heard the boxes moving.

"Yep. Just moved a box. Don't mind me. I think I'm ready to tap out if you'd like to give it a try."

Lila was fairly certain that she was the only target at the moment. None of the rest of the TPRA was involved in the magical world at all. While they lived for the paranormal, none of them had any real experience with the paranormal world outside of the ghost hunting they did. Lila knew there was far more out there than what went bump in the night—vampires, ghouls, and werewolves, just to name a few. She wasn't certain that zombies were really a thing, but she knew there was a fair amount of truth to any urban legend.

As she made her way down the ladder, she was extra careful to hang onto the rungs. Lila did not want to take any chances. The energy around her was not the most pleasant experience. Lila saw John looking up at her as she got to the bottom.

"Did you see any spiders, Lila? Don't lie to me." He looked super paranoid.

"No, I didn't see any spiders. The K2 did go off slightly, so there might be something up there. I just couldn't get a real feel for it. I'll stay down here if you want to give it a go."

Lila watched John head up the ladder and settled against the wall in the hallway. She sighed softly, knowing she wasn't going to get any peace until she traveled to Rainier, where she could look up Virginia Vinson to see what she could learn. Maybe the family had some kind of idea of what happened at the house. She resigned herself to making the trip as soon as possible, as long as she had enough money in her account to cover a week there. If she stayed at one of the smaller local motels, Lila could probably swing it. Lila would just have to make it work.

Chapter 4

Lila took a deep breath as she pulled into the drive of the small bed and breakfast that she had found just outside Rainier — Knight's Orchard. From the pictures on the website, it was a charming place to stay, which would be a treat for her. With the free Wifi and complimentary breakfast, Lila could hardly pass on it, especially since it wasn't breaking the bank.

Opening the car door, Lila stepped out of the car. A small wave of apprehension worked its way up her spine, maybe because she knew the woods here led to the one place she would only visit as a last resort. Witch's Hollow. Lila wasn't sure how she would react if she did find herself standing near the ley lines, powerful lines of magic that converged to form a vortex of energy that had been used for good and for evil. It wasn't that she was scared of it, just that she was cautious by nature. That was just who she was.

Lila left her suitcase in the trunk. She wanted to check in first and figure out where her room was. As she made her way up to the stairs, a toddler came racing around a corner and plowed into her. Lila lost her footing and fell over backwards, catching the little girl before she toppled over and injured herself.

The giggling girl touched her face and called behind her. "Karkar."

"Car?" Lila asked her curiously.

"No, that would be me."

Lila looked up at the mysterious voice and gasped aloud. "It's you."

"Why yes, it's me. Karter, that delinquent's uncle. Do I know you?" He looked at her curiously.

Lila cleared her throat. "I'm sorry. I just thought.... Never mind."

The toddler pushed away from her slightly and reached for her uncle's hand. "Karkar."

Lila took that moment to stand up and brush some of the dirt from her. She smiled at the little girl. "Hi. I'm Lila."

"Sophie." She reached for Lila's hand.

Lila could not resist her charm. She took the little girl's hand, but when she pushed Lila's hand into Karter's, Lila felt the earth shift under her feet. Closing her eyes, she saw the mysterious would be lover who was taking over her dreams. She shivered slightly and opened her eyes to find his blue eyes probing hers.

"Mate, mate, mate!" Sophie jumped around, clapping her hands.

Karter jerked his hand away as if he had been burned by her touch. He rubbed his fingers and scooped Sophie into his arms. "You little scamp."

"Mate, mate, mate!" Sophie chanted again.

A younger woman came out the front door and looked over at the child. "Soph, what are you going on about?"

"Mate, mate, mate." Sophie giggled as the woman retrieved her. "Karkar mate."

"Oh dear, Sophie. I'm so sorry, she's a little wound up. Someone gave her chocolate." She narrowed her eyes on Karter. "I'm Brina, and you must be Ms. Dawson?"

"Yes. Am I too early?" She drew her arms in closer to her body as she saw Karter's eyes roaming over her curiously.

"Not at all. Welcome to Knight's Orchard. Karter will be more than happy to get your bags for you if you'd like. Right, Karter?"

"Say what?" He cleared his throat as if he were a little distracted. "Happy to help. I just need the keys."

"Sure. There are a few bags in the trunk." She held her hand open with the keys. When Karter's fingers touched her skin, she flinched slightly and a flash of all the wicked things he had done in her dreams with those very same fingers made her blush from head to toe. When his hand stayed longer than necessary, she saw a golden light seem to flash across his eyes.

"Karter?" Brina tapped him on the shoulder.

"What? Oh, right." He took the keys and turned around, grumbling about something Lila could not hear as he went to retrieve her things.

"I could have gotten them myself—I mean, if he was too busy." Lila suddenly felt dowdy compared to the beautiful woman before her. Motherhood certainly agreed with her. And Lila had a feeling that she was already expecting her next, even though it wasn't visible yet. "Congratulations. I'm sure this one will be happy to have a sister...oh dear. Did I just say that?"

"See, I knew it was another girl!" Brina squealed with delight.

Lila blinked. "I...I mean, I don't usually —"

"Ms. Dawson, nothing surprises me. Plus, you're a witch from head to toe, dear. It does take one to know one. You're going to fit in just fine here. Yes, ma'am. Come inside."

Lila breathed a sigh of relief. She had no idea why she had blurted that out, but sometimes her intuition took over and she could not control herself. Grandma Tilly had always told her to bite her tongue sometimes, but Lila had never learned how, apparently.

She followed Brina into the house and smiled as she looked around at the warm energy that surrounded her. This house was filled with love and light from top to bottom, with just a little hint of mystery.

"We are informal here at Knight's Orchard. We'll do our check in here." Brina pulled a laptop from the coffee table and turned it on. "We used to have it all in paper, but I convinced Amber to get that moved over a year ago. Amber runs the place. We all pitch in when we get a chance. She'll be back this evening. She's going to love you. Just check your information here."

"Well, I suppose she must love all her guests. That's her job, right?" Lila checked over the information on the screen and used her finger to sign on the screen.

Brina smiled secretively. "Precisely. I've put you in the purple room. You're going to love that room. It's right across from the bathroom, which unfortunately you share with the top floor. We've got plans to put in another one in soon, but the boys have been too busy with their careers lately."

"Oh, well, honestly I don't need much. I live in a small old house. Sometimes I'm lucky if the shower works. So sharing a working one, that's not a problem." Lila sighed as she remembered that she really needed to have a plumber come out and fix that soon, but she'd been so distracted lately.

"You'll get along fine here." Brina patted her on the hand, and while Lila thought it was odd, at the same time it was comforting. "Oh, here's Karter now with your things. He'll take you to your room."

Lila's heart stuck in her throat and she gulped slightly, for what she heard wasn't what Brina had actually said, she was sure of it. Lila thought she had said Karter would take her *in* her room, which would be highly inappropriate considering they didn't know each other. Even though, she was pretty sure she knew more about him than she should. Vivid details of the way his mouth touched her skin raced through her mind. She shook her head and saw him grinning at her, almost as if he knew his affect over her.

Lila followed him upstairs and almost bumped into him when he stopped at the first door. "Oh, sorry."

His blue eyes lit up as a grin slid across his face. "No worries, Ms. Dawson—"

"Lila," she interjected.

"Lila...." He looked like the wheels were turning in his head as he opened the door.

Lila glanced around the room, impressed with how clean and inviting the space was. "It's beautiful."

"Yes, you...yes, it is." Karter coughed slightly as he set the bags on the bed for her.

"Sorry?" Lila could have sworn he was saying she was beautiful, but that just didn't ring true for her. No one had ever...well, Tilly had called her beautiful, but she loved her. Grandmas were supposed to say that. Why would a handsome man like Karter say that about her? He probably had his pick of partners. Lila's gaze roamed up and down the length of him, wondering if reality was anything close to the dream version of him.

He turned to find her checking him out and stepped closer to her. Karter took her hand in his and brought it to his mouth. When his lips touched her skin, Lila almost fainted as a tingling sensation shot through her. She felt as if lightning would strike her down at any time, the electrical energy floating between them was so overwhelming.

"I...." Lila didn't know what to say. "You...I mean—"

His phone started to ring, and he pulled himself away. Pulling his cell phone out of his pocket, he looked over the text. "Damn it."

"Everything all right?" Her voice was soft, almost inaudible to her own ears, yet he had clearly heard it.

"No. Yes. I mean, it's fine. I just have to head into Glamz. Apparently, there's a slight shift issue."

"Glamz?" Lila said in surprise.

"My bar," Karter answered. "I have to go...how long are you staying?"

Lila wasn't sure why he wanted to know that. "A week. I think. It depends on where my research leads me."

"Good." Another ding on his phone, and he cursed under his breath and his eyes flashed again. Karter ran a hand through his blond hair and looked over at her one last time.

"I've got to go."

"Of course." She watched him start to leave the room, and she whispered his name so softly that she didn't think anyone else could hear her. "*Karter....*"

He turned around and walked back to her. Karter put his hand on her face and his eyes were trained on hers. His mouth was so close to hers that Lila was sure he was going to kiss her, but he did not. "Come with me?"

"I...."

Lila tried to find an answer inside her, but staring in his eyes had almost made her lose control over any of her thoughts. When his mouth came closer to hers, Lila closed the gap and welcomed his kiss. It was soft, not like the aggressive ones he had come to her with in her dreams. She felt as if she were floating off the ground by the time he broke the kiss. Lila could not even open her eyes — she was scared to see what his face would say. Having kissed very few men, Lila was not that experienced at it.

His fingers stroked her cheek and his next words surprised her. They were soft and controlled, yet part of him was struggling for control. "Look at me, Lila."

Fear kept her frozen in place, but she fought against it and finally opened her eyes. His face looked almost tortured. "Are you okay?"

He chuckled. "You're too sweet, Lila."

"Oh...I'm sorry." She looked away from him, sure it was his way of telling her that he was not attracted to her. What in the world had made her kiss him? She really needed to get a grip.

He ran a finger over her lip. "Come with me, Lila."

Every inch of her wanted to. "I can't."

"Why not?" he asked her softly.

"You're trouble." She stepped backward slightly and bit the bottom of her lip nervously.

He wasn't angry with her response. Instead, he laughed loudly. "Yes, yes, I am. You are a gem, Lila."

Lila watched him leave, suddenly wishing she had gone with him. Perhaps that wasn't what a good girl would do, but it was what every inch of her wanted. She walked over to the window and saw him look up at her. Holding her hand up, she waved to him and saw a grin flash over his face. Lila couldn't help but smile back at him. Watching him leave, she put a hand over her mouth and touched the place where he had kissed her.

"You're in trouble, girl." she whispered to herself.

Closing her eyes, she wondered what would be so wrong with feeling something besides loneliness for a change. Lila sighed and shook her head. That wasn't what she had come here for. It was best that she remember the dark entity that had marked her as its next target. The scratches on her back were proof. While most scratches would have started to scab over by now, these were still as red and raw as the day she received them, a constant reminder of the evil that was plaguing her.

Yes, it was time to get back to work. She pulled out her laptop and logged into the Wifi to see if she could find the hours to the local library. Tomorrow she would need to visit it so she could look over any articles that would lead her to the last descendant of the Vinson family—Virginia Vinson.

Chapter 5

When Lila finally made her way back downstairs, she couldn't help but hear the conversation coming from the first floor. She paused on the steps.

"So, Sophie called her his mate?" A male voice asked.

"Yes. I told you that girl would be trouble," Karter grumbled.

For a moment, she thought Karter was talking about her, but then she heard the other voice continue.

"Hey, it's not her fault she's got Brina's genes. Besides, it's about time you settled down."

"She's just not—"

"Like your other women?" Brina's voice seemed slightly condemning. "That's a blessing, believe me."

An older gentleman walked down the hallway and saw her standing on the stairs. "Well, hello there," he said, loud enough for the others to hear. "You must be Ms. Dawson."

She gave him a feeble smile. "Yes, sir. Um, I was just wondering where I might be able to find a bite to eat in town."

"Nonsense, we've plenty of food here. Come join us."

Lila shivered slightly, wondering if she could just sneak back upstairs. "I would really hate to intrude."

"Dear girl, please join us. I fear Amber cooked up enough for an army."

"Army my ass—you know how much these boys eat," a voice grumbled from the dining room.

"That would be my lovely wife, Amber. She's anxious to meet you."

"Me?" Lila squeaked. She crept slowly down the stairs and took the arm that he offered her. "Thank you."

"I'm Kenton Knight. You met Brina, my daughter-in-law, and my son, Karter." He guided her into the dining room.

Lila felt a dark blush staining her face as several pairs of eyes looked up at her. She kept her eyes trained to the floor, afraid to see the humor that must be painted on their faces. Lila took a deep breath and summoned the courage to look up. "Good evening."

"Welcome to Knight's Orchard," an older woman wished her. As Lila looked over her, she realized that she must be Amber Knight, but that wasn't all she noticed. The silver glittering pentacle at her throat brought Lila great comfort.

"Merry meet," she answered softly.

Amber Knight's eyes twinkled in surprise. "Yes, indeed, dear child."

Lila was reminded of her grandma, and for a brief moment her heart felt warmer than it had in quite some time. She wasn't sure what to say next, but she didn't have to figure that out, thank goodness.

"Sit."

Kenton beckoned her to a chair, which just happened to be opposite Karter. She hesitated slightly, mostly because she wasn't sure how she was going to get through a meal with him sitting across from her. As she sat down, she felt his eyes on her. Lila did her best to ignore him as she let the words from earlier run across her mind. Not like his other women. Lila could have told them that. They probably actually had some kind of experience with the opposite sex.

"So, you've met a few of the family," Amber said.

"Where's the little one?" Lila asked politely.

"She's sleeping. Sophie finally ran off all the sugar her uncle let her get into earlier. So sorry she knocked you over."

"Not at all. She's adorable," Lila assured her.

"Do you have any children in your family?" Brina asked her curiously.

"I'm not sure. Maybe...." Lila nibbled on her bottom lip. "I'm afraid we're estranged at the moment."

"I'm sorry to hear that," Brina replied. Her soft eyes were filled with concern.

"I don't exactly fit in with their definition of a Christian woman." Lila looked down at her fingers and realized that her nails were in serious need of attention.

"Their loss." Karter's voice was the first she heard.

Her eyes shot up to his and she was at a loss for words. She opened her mouth as if she was trying to think of what to say, but closed it and swallowed them deep inside. Lila was unsettled just by his presence. She nibbled her bottom lip and saw his eyes were now trained on them. Clearing her throat, she turned to Amber Knight.

"You have a lovely inn."

"Why, thank you, dear. It's been in the family for some time, and has served us all well. The boys all grew up here."

"Boys?" Lila looked around the table and saw the man sitting next to Brina.

"Killian. And that fool there, you know. Karter," Killian introduced himself.

"There's also Kam, Kyle, and Kendrick," Kenton interrupted.

"Wow. Five?" Lila was impressed. She turned to Amber. "How did you survive?"

Amber chuckled. "Lots of prayers and meditation. A little bit of luck, too."

"We weren't all bad," Karter disputed.

"No, we weren't. But then again, we had to counterbalance your mischief," Killian teased him.

Karter looked as if he were ready to leap over at his brother. "I wasn't *that* bad."

Lila smiled as she imagined a younger Karter running around the house. With those long lashes and his adorable pouting face, Lila was sure he had gotten away with quite a bit. When Karter turned back to face her, she tried to hide her amusement, but he clearly saw it.

His eyes glistened slightly as a rueful smile covered his face. "Okay. Maybe I was a little hellion."

"*Was?*" Killian choked on his water and his knee could be heard hitting the table. "Ouch, why did you...? Oh."

"You'll have to excuse, Killian. He tends to rile his brother up at any turn." Brina winked at her.

"I do not—" Another thump was heard. "Okay, maybe a little."

Lila smiled perceptively and glanced at Karter again. "He probably deserved it."

Karter's mouth opened to protest, but then he closed it thoughtfully. "You're probably right."

The rest of the table were looking at Karter as if he had lost his mind. Karter turned to look at them. "What?"

Killian was the first to speak. The corner of his mouth was turned up in a smile. "So, what brings you to the area?"

"Just some research." Lila wasn't sure she should give the exact details of her visit.

"On?" Karter asked her.

"Nothing that interesting. Just some descendants of Benjamin Vinson."

"Virginia?" Amber asked curiously.

"Uh...yeah." How in the world did she know that so easily? "Did you know her?"

"Of course I do. That old bat is still alive and kicking. She's what...seventy-eight now?" Amber asked her husband.

"Amber, darling, we don't refer to people as old bats." Kenton must have seen the shock on Lila's face.

"We do when they want to be called that. I'm sorry if that seemed crass, but Virginia often refers to herself as a dingbat. Something to do with her blood lines."

"Oh." Lila was relieved to hear that. "Do you know where I can find her?"

"I do. Rainier Homestead. It's a retirement home. I'm sure Karter could take you there in the morning if you wanted."

"Mother...." Karter's voice almost growled at his mother.

"Well, you know her pretty well too. Didn't she sell you that doll?" Amber's voice was filled with fake innocence.

Even Lila saw through it, though she pretended not to notice anything.

"You have a doll?" For some reason, Lila found this information intriguing.

"No, *I* do not have a doll." Karter seemed to think she was implying that he collected dolls or something. "It's at the club. Glamz is a —"

"Paranormal night club?" answered Lila.

"You've heard of it?" Karter asked with an appreciative smile.

"Of course I have." Lila watched a cocky smile appear on his face, and knew he thought she was admiring him, but she had to set him straight. "It's irresponsible, what you're doing."

His face seemed to blanch slightly. "Excuse me?"

"Haunted items can sometimes attach negative energy onto innocent people. Have you considered the repercussions?"

"I...." Karter looked as if he were trying to come up with an argument.

"Lost your words, Karter?" Killian teased him. "Hey, don't you...? Ow. Bri!"

"I didn't mean to be rude," Lila apologized, but realized it might be too late. She squeezed her eyes shut and pushed away from the table. "Excuse me."

Lila left the dining room and was desperate to find any exit. She found the front door and made her way toward it. When she closed it behind her, she gasped in the cold air around her, hoping it would clear her thoughts. She started to walk, not knowing her destination, only that she wanted to be anywhere but there right now. The stars lit her path as she walked across the orchard. When she found a small bench, she sat down and realized that tears were falling down her face.

Until this moment, Lila hadn't truly realized how lonely her life had been. The Knights were filled with so much love and life that she was reminded of a time in her life when she'd had all those things. It had seemed like a much simpler time then, before she understood the bigotry that had run through her entire family.

She brought her knees up to her chest and put her head on her arms. Looking up at the stars, Lila sighed. Right now, she was wishing she had never walked into the Vinson house. It would have been far easier if she had never come to this place. To find herself face to face with her dream lover was humiliating. Lila could never measure up to the women he'd known before her. Now she was even wondering if his kiss had even happened, or if she had completely conjured it. Lila sniffed slightly and put her head on her arms again as melancholy settled in to keep her company.

"Lila...."

She didn't look up, convinced that she had just imagined his voice, for Lila had not heard the sound of any footsteps. "Go away."

"Lila, look at me."

She turned to the sound of his voice and gasped. "You are really here."

He grinned at her. "You can pinch me if you like."

Lila opened her mouth and shut it before she said another word. "Why *are* you here?"

"Because I have nowhere else to be."

"Oh...I see." Lila's lip wobbled slightly. He had nothing better to do. That was just great. She turned back away from him.

"Damn it." Karter sat down on the bench next to her. "There's something about you that makes me lose my mind, Lila."

She pursed her lips. "Is that a compliment?"

"Do you want one?" He asked her with a charming smile.

"I'm not sure that's wise." Lila held a hand up to ward him off slightly.

"Why not?"

"I'm not likely to believe you," she answered softly. That, and the fact that she wouldn't know a real compliment if it bit her in the...well...anywhere really.

Karter's face looked at her seriously. "You're a breath of fresh air, Lila."

She drew her lips together and shook her head at him. "I'm not. Everything about me is stagnant."

His hand reached for hers. "Lila...."

Her eyes met his and she was lost inside them for a moment, reminded of a mysterious man who was one with the beast inside him. "I didn't come here for this."

"Didn't you?" He asked her softly as he brought her hand to his mouth again.

She tried to pull away from him, but she was entranced by him. "Karter, please don't—"

"What?"

"You'll only make it worse." Lila finally managed to pull her hand away.

"What, Lila?" Karter's eyes were flashing with golden

lights as he battled something inside him.

Closing her eyes, she shook her head. She pushed away from the bench and crossed her arms over her chest as she looked up at the stars. Why in the world would destiny throw him into her path so cruelly? It was bad enough she dreamt about him, knowing that when she woke up no man like him would ever want someone like her.

Karter's arms slid around her stomach. He pulled her against him and kissed the top of her head. "I'm drawn to you, Lila. In ways you cannot understand, not yet."

"The beast inside?" she whispered.

Karter flinched at her words. "How do you...?"

Lila sighed. "You wouldn't believe me if I told you."

"Try me."

She turned in his arms and looked up at him. "For the past year, my dreams have been filled with you and him."

"What exactly do you dream about?" he asked her curiously.

"You and the wolf, you both chase me until you finally catch me." Lila was leaving out a lot, but she was afraid to speak it.

"And what happens when I catch you?" His mouth was so close to hers that his breath tickled her lips.

She gasped slightly. "I...excuse me."

Lila pushed away from him and started to make her way back up the path, knowing that he was walking right behind her. She fought the urge to run. Her heart was racing so fast that she was almost having trouble breathing.

Karter's arm reached out to grab hers. "Did I hurt you?"

Lila saw the desperation in his eyes. He was worried.

"No, it's not like that, Karter."

"Then what is it?"

"I...I'm afraid of what happens next."

"Why?"

"Because I've never done it before." Lila looked down at the ground.

"I'm sorry?" Karter was clearly confused.

"Please don't make me say it." Tears started to fall down her face as embarrassment flooded through her.

Karter finally seemed to catch on to what she was implying. "You're a *virgin*? All the women in the world, and he chooses a virgin?"

His laughter ripped through her like a jagged shard. She stomped on his foot and slapped him across the face. Then Lila ran as fast as her feet would carry her, not caring if he followed her or not. She heard him calling after her, but she was so angry that she refused to listen. When two arms grabbed her from behind, she fought him tooth and nail. She turned in his arms and tried to pummel him with her fists, and tripped over a root that was sticking out from the dirt. The two of them toppled over and the breath was knocked from her lungs. She was gasping for air when his lips came down on hers.

Lila was transported to another time and place, filled with the memories of hundreds of kisses she'd had before, none of which had been real flesh and blood like the man who was on top of her. She wanted to push him away, but her hands seemed to pull him closer. By the time he broke the kiss, Lila was under a spell she couldn't seem to fight. "Please...."

"Yes, Lila?"

"Let me up." She was fighting for any sense of control. She needed to get away from him, before it was too late.

Karter struggled to rein himself in and looked as if he would reject her request, but instead, he surprised her. "As you wish."

As soon as Karter moved, Lila sat up next to him. "I'm sorry."

"You're sorry?" Karter was confused.

"To disappoint you." She looked up at the stars again and blinked away a tear. Why couldn't the damn house have sent her somewhere else? If she had just booked a different hotel, then this would never have happened.

"Disappoint...what are you going on about?" Karter ran a hand through his hair. "Because you're a virgin?"

"I didn't mean to throw myself at you. It was just a dream. Probably just a stu—"

"Don't finish that," Karter warned her.

"I—"

"Lila...shut up." His eyes flashed their warning.

"That's not very nice!" she chided him.

"Neither are his thoughts. And while I have some morals where virgins are concerned, my beast...he doesn't care."

Lila's eyes narrowed on him. "I don't understand."

"I don't suspect you do." He put a hand to her cheek and sighed. "Let's get you back inside. I'm sure my mother will have quite a few words for me. Time to face the music."

Lila blushed. "I don't suppose I could just eat in my room?"

"I'll bring you something."

"That's okay. I can get it myself." She held her hand up

in protest.

"Relax. I don't go around ravishing our guests." Karter grinned at her.

"That's a relief." It wasn't though. His words just made her feel that he had found her lacking. That was no surprise to Lila.

She was about to push up from the ground when he pulled her into his lap. His mouth captured hers in a kiss that was filled with something she could not quite understand. When his tongue slid inside her mouth, Lila shook slightly. A longing that had only been a remnant of her fading dreams was now awake inside her, as the reality was so much better than the dream version of him. The more he kissed her, the harder it was to see any kind of reason.

When he broke the kiss, he cradled her against his body. Lila had trouble figuring out whose breathing was more ragged. He seemed just as affected by their kiss as she was. She took a chance and let her hand slide against his face. Sparks filtered between them the moment she did, a feeling that was becoming familiar to her.

Lila sighed. "We should get back."

"Yes." His voice seemed reluctant, but he did release her from his arms and let her stand up. He led her up the path to the house, but before he let her enter he whispered her name. "Lila...?"

"Yes, Karter?"

"I'm glad you're a virgin." He grinned at her.

"And just why is that?" She asked him quietly.

He moved closer to her ear and whispered, "Because when I make you mine, no one else will ever have you."

His words made her shiver in the darkness as he walked away from her and let himself inside the house. Lila had a feeling things were about to get even more interesting. Could she allow herself to fall into his arms? There was still so much she needed to do. She couldn't afford the distraction, but neither could she avoid it. Lila knew she was trapped somewhere between heaven and hell. How in the world was she going to survive this?

Chapter 6

When Karter made his way into the kitchen his mother was shaking her head at him. Karter refused to meet her eyes, but that didn't stop her from going off on him anyway.

"You're such an idiot." Amber clucked her tongue at him. "She's a good girl too, Karter. If you ruin her—"

"I would never...." Karter tried to argue with her, but his mother was hell bent on tearing him a new asshole. Karter shut his mouth and just let her blow. It would be far easier for him, even if it was entertaining his brother. Killian was holding back his laughter, Karter was sure of it.

"It's high time you found yourself a decent mate to settle down with, Karter. You can't go sowing your wild oats for too much longer. You know how this works." Amber crossed her arms over her chest and closed her eyes. Then she opened them and rolled them up to the ceiling. "I just don't know where I went wrong."

"Mother!" Karter had finally had enough of the tirade. "Stop. You can't choose my mate for me. Only we can. And he's—"

"Smitten," Brina said intuitively.

Karter opened his mouth and closed it. He looked down at the table and pushed his food on his plate as he waited for Killian to bring it home with one of his famous zingers. Instead, his brother did the opposite.

"It's a hell of a thing, isn't it?" Killian asked him softly.

"What, no jokes? Just get them over with." Karter gestured for the hits to start coming.

"It's not funny." Killian sighed. "Let's go for a walk."

"I don't think so." Karter didn't trust him as far as he could throw him. "Besides, I'm supposed to bring her some food."

"I'll do it." Amber held up a hand. "Can't have you scaring the poor thing."

"Why do you think I can't keep it in my pants?" Amber's eyes narrowed on him accusingly, and Karter had the decency to blush. "Okay, wrong question. But I would think my own mother would be on my side."

"That girl is skittish, Karter. If you push too hard, she's liable to run," Amber cautioned him. "Besides, I like her. She reminds me of someone I used to know."

"Who's that?" Killian asked her curiously.

"Me." Amber pushed away from the table and took her plate with her.

"Really? I think there's part of the story you left out, Dad." Karter gazed at his father perceptively.

"Aren't you going on a walk?" Kenton asked him with a half-grin on his face.

"Fine." Karter took one large bite of food and swallowed

it down with a gulp of water before he pushed away from the table. He carried his plate to the sink and kissed his mother on the cheek before he turned away.

He knew she meant well, but this wasn't something she could meddle in. Hadn't she learned that the hard way when she tried to get in between Killian and Brina? When the beast was engaged, there was nothing and no one that could stop him from going after what he wanted. Even if Karter wanted to protest, his beast would overrule him without giving it a second thought.

As Karter left the back of the house, he let his wolf take over. His body contorted and shifted until his skin was covered with fur, hands replaced with paws, his nails with claws. He raced across the woods as fast as his four legs could carry him. By the time he made it to their usual meeting place, his wolf was panting. His wolf howled in the moonlight, a lone pitiful howl of a creature longing for something just out of its reach.

When he shifted back into his human form, Karter looked up at the moon whose magic had always ruled his life. From the time he had first changed as a hormonal teenager, the wolf had been a constant companion. Up until this point, both had been living a wilder life, refusing to settle down with just any woman. At twenty-eight, Karter was still young enough to be a bachelor for a while, and that had suited him just fine. Now that his wolf had found its mate, that was no longer an option. He would no longer be able to prowl.

Prowling. It was the ability to move from woman to woman without the added pressure of settling down. For a time, they had been unable to prowl. That was because their alpha had not chosen a mate. Thankfully, Killian finally chose Brina, which made it fair game for the rest of them to sow their oats with no repercussions. Kam was the only one who was unable to prowl. Not because he had found his mate, but because she seemed to elude him. Karter felt bad for him. A life without sex was not a life worth living.

"Shit." Karter shook his head in frustration.

"Problem, brother?" Killian asked him.

"She's a virgin, Killian."

"Oh?" His voice was filled with humor.

"Don't even start."

"Well, that's a first." Killian could not seem to contain his laughter.

"What in the hell am I supposed to do with a virgin, Killian?" He let out a long sigh.

"Well, the body parts work the same, Karter. You just...." Killian scratched his head and looked up at the sky. "Yeah. I got nothing. Maybe you should ask Kam."

"No fucking way am I asking him." Karter shook his head. "And you better not say anything either. She didn't even want to tell me."

"You didn't try to...." Killian didn't finish his sentence.

"I do have some control, Killian. I'm not that much of a player."

"And you've never slept with a...."

"No way. They get too many notions in their heads when you're their first. Besides, I enjoy sex, Killian. I want a woman with—"

"Experience?" Killian offered.

"Yes. But there's something about her that makes me

crazy." Karter shook his head. "I don't know what to do."
It was true. Karter was divided between the part of him that
wanted to make her completely off limits and the part of him
that wanted to show her what she'd been missing all these
years. The problem was, none of it seemed to be up to him. If
he wasn't careful, though, he would scare her off.

"There is no denying it, Karter. When you know, you
know."

"Was it like that with Brina?" Karter asked him curiously.

"Don't you remember me wanting to rip your head off
for just looking at her? I would have ripped you limb from
limb if you had even tried anything."

Karter chuckled. "I probably would have deserved it."

"Perhaps, but the emotions racing through you won't
make any sense. Every second you are away from her, you'll
both be looking for her. Her scent, her touch, her taste. You
won't get enough...I still can't."

"That might be a tiny bit of an overshare." Karter held his
hand up. He certainly didn't want to imagine Killian doing
the nasty with Brina right now. Not that he hadn't found her
attractive at the time, but he had known even then that Brina
was off limits. They all had.

"I can't believe you get the virgin, though." Killian
snickered slightly. "You're probably the most promiscuous
out of all of us."

"That's fair," Karter agreed. His bed was never lacking
companions. Like last week, when the blonde and her friend
had offered to.... A snarl ripped through his brain as his wolf
threw up a barrier. "What the fuck?"

"Let me guess—tried to imagine another woman?"

Killian asked him knowingly. "Just an FYI...none of them exist anymore."

"Well, fuck. That's just messed up." Karter kicked at the dirt. "There was a redhead who... what did she do again?"

Killian laughed aloud and slapped him on the shoulder. "It's a hell of a thing, isn't? Don't worry, it will be worth it."

"She's not like the others, Killian. I have to be careful with her. Bring her around slowly, I think." Karter looked up at the moon. "She's not just going to fall into my arms. It's going to take a little work."

"Nothing is worth having if it isn't worth fighting for, Karter. When you find your mate, you fight like hell to keep her. Even if it means you have to put your needs aside to do it." Killian looked up at the sky. "Sometimes you don't have to compromise yourself at all. Sometimes you have to grow up."

"I'm twenty-eight, Killian. I'm not a child."

"No, you're not. But you look like a kid who lost his favorite toy."

"Well, I wasn't expecting to find my mate tonight. I was still on the prowl. It's not like what happened to you. Although, you didn't prowl as much as some of us did."

"No one prowled as much as you did, Karter."

Karter kept his mouth shut. He liked sex. Did that make him a bad person? He was always careful to choose the women who weren't looking for relationships, because he knew one day he would have to settle down. Unless his wolf was on board, he would be leading them down a dead-end road. It might make him appear to be a player, but he was not as careless as people made him out to be. "How do I know this is real?"

"What does she smell like?"

"Vanilla."

"What color are her eyes?"

"Brown with a few hazel specks."

"Anything else?"

"She has twenty small freckles on her face." Which made him wonder what other parts of her body had freckles. He assumed the places that were untouched by the sun would be a creamy white. Unless she bathed in the sun. As he imagined searching for freckles down the curve of her neck to her breasts, the milky white image he conjured made his cock spring to life. He clenched his hands into fists and let out a slow breath.

"You had enough time to count her freckles?" Killian whistled in amazement. "That's...."

"Pathetic?" Karter waited for his brother to tease him some more.

"No, impressive. I don't think I would have been able to recall that about Brina from one night. You've spent less than an hour in her presence."

"She has one freckle on the back of her left ear, too." One that he had been tempted to lick when he whispered into it. He tried to contain the shudder that moved through his body. This was going to be a lot harder than he'd thought.

"Yep. You've got it bad. I don't think you have ever described any of your past girlfriends, Karter. Besides body parts, you barely share anything personal about them."

"Her tears, Killian, they're...." Karter didn't know how to describe it.

"Like gut punches?"

"Yes." They hurt like hell to see. The fact that he had been the reason for them made him sick to his stomach.

"You'll find it gets easier to handle those over time. Especially when they're pregnant. They cry at everything." Killian shook his head sadly.

"If only...." The idea of Lila carrying his offspring inside her made his heart thump louder in his chest. She would be the only woman he would ever want those with. And judging by the way his beast howled inside him, the sooner the better. He turned to look at Killian. "Thank you."

"Yep. I'm still tempted to tell Kam." His eyes twinkled merrily.

"You'd embarrass my mate like that?" Karter felt the hair rise on the back of his neck as his eyes flashed their warning.

"No, I would not. Relax, Karter. You're going to need your strength, I think." Killian swatted him on the back again. "We'd better get back before Mother sends the others after us."

"Agreed." Besides, Karter was already plotting a seduction in his head. Lila would be his, no matter what it took. While he was not the most patient man, Karter would find a way to slow his roll just a little. The end game would be worth it.

Chapter 7

Lila heard a knock on her door and her heart almost stopped beating in her chest. She opened the door and found Amber Knight standing outside with a tray of food. Trying to hide her disappointment, she offered her a small smile. "Hello."

"Karter thought you might be hungry." Amber brought the food to the small bureau dresser.

"Thank you." Lila found the woman's presence comforting.

"He's a little too much to handle from time to time, but he means well." Amber touched her arm gently and then pulled back. "You're being followed?"

Lila closed her eyes and bit her lip. "Yes. It's a long story."

"Sit, child. Tell me all about it." Amber put her hand on Lila's back and saw her wince. "You're injured. Let me help you."

Lila lifted her shirt and let Amber take a look. "It refuses to heal."

55

"I can fix that. As soon as you tell me what happened." Amber led her to bed and patted the mattress.

"I'm sorry. I shouldn't have brought this here." Lila looked up at the ceiling. "I hear spirits. For the most part, I try to help them move on to their afterlives."

"It's a true calling for you."

"I also help an investigative team from time to time. They're the closest thing I have to friends." Lila put a hand to her mouth. "I'm not sure why I told you that. I must sound awfully needy and—"

"Not at all, Lila. I think you're quite refreshing. Perhaps lonely too."

Her lips wobbled. "Oh dear. See, I didn't think so. Well, I knew I was, but it wasn't until I saw your wonderful family that I realized I was missing quite a bit in my life."

Amber put a hand on her shoulder. "It's their loss, child."

"Except they all have each other and…well, all I had was Grandma Tilly. She's gone now too." Lila shook away the pain that was always close to the surface. "Goodness, I'm like a wet mop."

"Believe me, the Knight men will do that to you. Something I know firsthand."

"What? No, Karter hasn't done anything," Lila tried to defend him.

"Yet. Give him time, dear. He'll do something to make you rip your hair out and then offer you a sunny smile the next minute. He's just like his father in that way."

Lila giggled despite herself. What Amber Knight described was something she could see happening, if she allowed herself to get attached to him. But Lila wasn't letting herself get caught up in any kind of entanglement with him, even though every inch of her was aware of the way he made her feel.

"So, you were ghost hunting," Amber reminded her.

Lila was happy for the redirect. She didn't like where her mind was heading. "Yes. John finally got clearance from the new owners to let us investigate the Vinson House. Strange things had been happening there for almost a century now. I had no idea what we were walking into. That thing inside, it's like nothing I've ever seen before. He's enslaved the spirits in the house. It's like they're tethered there under his control. He didn't seem to like me at all."

"These are demonic scratches?" Amber pursed her lips together thoughtfully. "Have you saged?"

"Seven times. I've used every oil I could find to heal these. Nothing seems to work. They're not getting worse, but the wounds refuse to heal." Lila didn't know what she could do to change that. There was very little left in her own arsenal of tricks and everything that Tilly had taught her. "I'm afraid my resources are as limited as my experience."

"There's nothing wrong with that, my dear." Amber patted her hand comfortingly.

"I'm just a solitary...." Lila looked at the ground, ashamed of the fact that she was alone in that too.

"So what? Most of us are. Many of the women at the camp are on their own too. Our beliefs are vast and ever changing, but one thing holds us close together."

"The rede?" Lila suggested. The rede was a rule that all of them upheld.

"Do what you will, so long as it harms none. Most of us

uphold that above all else. So, this thing, he has his hooks in you, love." Amber clucked her tongue. "We'll have to do something about that."

"You can help me?" Lila was surprised. She was starting to think the only thing that could help her was to get rid of the demon who had created it.

"It will take some time, but yes, I do believe I can. Has it gotten infected at all?" Amber asked her.

"No. I keep it cleaned the best that I can. I need to get rid of this. It's how he tracks me." Lila shivered as she remembered the angry being that was lurking in the shadows. She didn't feel him so much as his minions. The fact that she might have brought them here did not escape her.

"Don't worry, Lila. This house is well protected. Brina and I both keep the darkness away."

"Brina is a witch too?" Lila's eyes shot up in surprise.

"Well, of course she is. A mighty fine one, too. We'll figure something out. Until then, I do think you're right to talk to the old bat, but let's keep you protected, shall we?" Amber took her necklace off and handed it to her.

"I can't take this from you." Lila tried to hand it back to her.

"You must not refuse a gift from another witch, Lila. It's bad form," Amber teased her.

"Oh, I'm sorry. I didn't mean to sound ungrateful." Lila let out a long sigh. "I starting to feel like there's a lot about the world I never learned."

"I think I actually admire your innocence. It's a powerful thing to wield. The dark is attracted to it, but cannot touch it. He may have marked you, but he will never be able to destroy you. That I guarantee. You have nothing to fear."

Perhaps, but it wasn't her that Lila was concerned about now. What if that thing did follow her, and attacked the Knight family just for allowing her into their home? Especially that darling child? Lila knew she had to do something about that. Tomorrow, she would find another place to stay. She couldn't stay here and put them at risk like that.

"Well, I'll leave you to eat. I'll look through my books to see what I can do to help you heal those." Amber smiled softly at her. "I really am happy you chose to stay with us. The universe works in mysterious ways."

As Amber Knight walked from the room, Lila thought she heard her say that she was just what Karter needed. She sighed and closed her eyes. Karter was...confusing. The kind of man who wouldn't have given her a second thought anywhere else in the world. Maybe that was because Lila had never learned how to step out of her shell. Or maybe she just had too many other things to do with her life.

While in college, she had been on a mission to prove she could do it all on her own, especially when her family had withdrawn all of their support. After college, that's when Grandma Tilly had found her. She'd forever be thankful for that. And then when Tilly got sick, Lila had been consumed with taking care of her. There simply hadn't been any time to live her life. Not that right now was any better. As much as every inch of her wanted to see what it would be like to fall into Karter's arms, to shut her mind off and just feel, Lila couldn't let herself do that. If she did, she would never want to leave.

She shivered as she remembered his words — when he

made her his, no one else would ever have her. That was probably true, but she did not want to stick around long enough for him to tire of her. His playboy smile and wicked ways would eventually remind him what he was missing. But still, just a taste. It would last her the rest of her life.

Lila looked at the food on the plate. She had been hungry earlier, but now her mind was too filled with thoughts that could not be put to rest. Nibbling a few bites, she pushed the rest of the food across the plate before she walked over to the window. Gazing outside, she saw two wolves racing across the ground. When one of them stopped and turned to look up at her, Lila held a hand up and touched the window with her fingertips. As he turned away, Lila watched him start to run after the other wolf. Sadness filtered through her as she whispered his name. "*Karter.*"

The wolf stopped in its tracks and turned around to look up at her again. Her breath stopped in her chest as she let the curtain fall back into place. Had he heard her? That was impossible, right? "Stop it, Lila. Now you're just imagining things."

She went to her luggage and found one of her flannel night gowns. Taking her toiletries with her, she decided to take a quick shower. Sometimes when she was out of sorts, a hot shower helped her wash them away. It couldn't hurt.

Checking the hallway to make sure no one else was lurking in the shadows, she quickly raced to the bathroom. As she washed the day from her skin, her scratches stung. She winced, but made herself tolerate it. The only way to keep them from being infected was to keep them clean.

By the time she was done, Lila's fingers were slightly

pruned over. Drying off, she quickly dressed into her clothes and brushed her hair. The steam from the shower had fogged up the mirror. Wiping her hand across it, she looked at herself. The same plain girl she'd always been. Nothing she could do about that. Lila sighed.

Walking across the hall to her room, Lila opened the door and slid inside. She went to the bed and pulled the covers away, but didn't crawl into the bed right away. She moved to the window and looked outside again, searching for the only thing her heart desired. When she didn't see him there, her face fell in disappointment.

"Looking for me?" Karter called to her from across the room.

Lila jumped at the sound of his voice and gasped in shock. She put her hand on her heart and tried to keep it from leaping out of her chest. "What are you doing here? How did you...?"

"You called for me," he whispered across the divide.

"I shouldn't have done that." Lila turned back to the window and looked outside, trying to distract herself from what her heart truly wanted right now.

"I will always come when you call, Lila."

His mouth was close to her ear again, and she couldn't help wondering how he could move so effortlessly. The heat of his breath on her neck made her shiver in the dark. His tongue snaked out and licked just behind her ear, and she heard him groan behind her. Lila felt a jolt of something electrified within her. Was it nerve endings firing for the first time? She couldn't be sure, but she was afraid of it nonetheless.

Lila turned around to face him, and was surprised by the

look on his face. Was that longing? "What are you doing here, Karter?"

"A good night kiss?" He grinned at her.

"Just a kiss?" She almost squeaked, because his hands had slid down her back and over her behind in a far too intimate way.

"A kiss, fair Lila."

As if anything could ever be just anything with him. Lila took a chance anyway. She looked into the oceans of his eyes and found a universe hidden inside. When his mouth came down on hers, he took her breath away. Her arms seemed to have a mind of their own as they slid up over his shoulders and wrapped around his neck. She pulled him in closer, knowing this might very well be the last time she kissed him. Tomorrow, she would be out of his life forever. If only she could take more of him with her.

When he broke the kiss, Lila kept her eyes closed. She was afraid to see the look on his face. His fingers stroked her lips and she sighed softly. They trailed down her face and her head dipped back in reflex. When his mouth slid to the curve of her neck, she felt his teeth against her skin, as if he were going to bite her. When he stepped away from her Lila turned to see him fighting some kind of internal battle.

"Are you okay, Karter?" Lila reached her hand out to him, but he jumped back in reflex.

"Good night, Lila."

She watched him leave the room and bit her lip. Had she done something wrong? Had he realized how short she came up when he measured her against everyone from his past? Lila sat on the edge of her bed and looked down at her feet.

Her back burned as if a new fire had been lit against it. Tears stung her eyes. It was time to move on in the morning. She couldn't let this thing attack any of the Knight family the way it had her.

Chapter 8

That night Lila tossed and turned, haunted by the face of the one man who set her soul aflame. Until now, she'd never had a name for the face. Karter smiled at her before he ran his fingers down her spine. Her flesh tingled in her sleep as if his hands really strummed against her. When his mouth ran hot kisses down her neck, she felt him pause again as if deliberating whether or not to linger. Instead, he moved down to the valley of her breasts, and just as always, Lila awoke.

"Why does it always have to stop there?" Lila sighed, and turned around to look at the alarm clock. Six in the morning. Now was as good a time as any. She scribbled her note to the Knight family and left the pentacle that Amber had been so generous to give her with the full deposit for her stay. Lila thanked them for being so kind to her, but said that she couldn't bother them with her troubles.

There was more to it, though. She wasn't just protecting them. If Lila was honest with herself, she was running from the one thing that frightened her the most. Karter. He had the ability to completely destroy her, and right now, if she didn't put distance between them, Lila would let him. She quietly packed her things and dressed for the day.

When she was finished, she walked to the window and looked out one last time, almost wishing she saw the lone wolf standing outside. She would spend the rest of her life dreaming about him, that she was sure of, but forgetting her would be second nature to him. As she walked down the stairs, she was careful not to disturb anyone who might be sleeping inside the inn.

Thankfully, she was able to slip away with little notice. Considering how loud her car was, that was a feat in itself. Today, she would try to find her way to the Rainier Homestead and find what out what she could from Virginia Vinson. Then she would figure out what to do from there.

Lila drove the distance to Rainier, and was pleasantly surprised by the charm of the small town as the first morning rays shone down on the older buildings. She couldn't imagine what it must have been like to grow up such a small town, where everyone knew everyone else. Did that mean the town of Rainier knew all about the secret the of the Knight pack? Lila was pretty sure that all of the men were werewolves, just like Karter. It must be something that ran deep in their family.

At seven, very few things were open, except for the small diner on the corner of Main and Elm. Lila parked her car out front and went inside to get herself a bite to eat. She sat down at one of the tables and took out the menu that was folded on the side. She was so absorbed in the menu she did not see anyone slide into the booth across from her.

"What looks good?" He asked her quietly.

Lila dropped the menu and her mouth fell open. She shook her head and looked down at her hands. "What are you doing here?"

"That's a good question. The better question is, why did you run?" His eyes were cool and collected.

"What might I get the two of...? Oh, hello, Karter." The waitress gave him a wink as her shoulder came up flirtatiously. "I haven't seen you in a while."

"I've been busy."

Lila pursed her lips as a jealous bug seemed to buzz in her ear. That was before she reminded herself she had nothing to be jealous of. She had no claim to him at all. "I'll have the pancake platter, please. Scrambled eggs. Orange juice and water, please."

The woman blinked and turned to look at Lila. "Of course, sweetie. And what about you, darling?"

"I'll have the same." Karter dismissed her with a charming smile. When she walked away, he reached for Lila's hand.

Lila pulled her hand away from his. She couldn't afford to let him touch any of her. If he did, she would break her resolve. "Please don't."

"Lila, look at me."

"I'd rather not." She turned to look out the window instead. Why was he here? He should have just let her go. He would be wasting his time with her.

"So...why did you leave, Lila?" He asked her softly.

"I have my reasons." She did. They had seemed so resolute just a few moments ago, but just hearing his silky voice made her want to throw herself into his arms. Arms that had probably held every attractive woman in this county.

Karter slid her money across the table with the necklace she had left behind. She looked down at it and closed her eyes. When her eyes looked up at his, she didn't see the amusement she thought she would. Instead, she saw a softness that seemed almost foreign to her.

"You can't run, Lila."

"Oh? Why not?" She crossed her arms around her.

"I'll always find you." Golden light flashed across his eyes, and Lila's breath caught in her throat.

"Why would you say that?" She shook her head at him.

"You'll understand soon enough."

"Doubtful." She chewed on her bottom lip and heard him suck in his breath.

"Stop that, Lila."

"Stop...what?" Her eyes flew up to his and the softness she thought she had seen before was filled with something hard and determined. Her nibbling resumed and she saw his face harden. She put her hand to her lips and blocked them from view.

"Here are your drinks." The waitress sat them down on the table and made sure to overextend herself so that her cleavage was in plain sight.

Lila snorted softly, assuming that Karter would be checking them out. He was a man, after all. She was surprised to find his eyes had not left her face. Lila couldn't resist drawing her bottom lip inside her mouth one last time before she looked up at the waitress. "So, are you two old friends?"

"You could say that. Karter and me, we go way back, don't we, sugar?" The woman slid her arm around Karter's shoulders.

Lila pursed her lips together. It was clear that the woman did not see her as any kind of competition. Not that she blamed her—Lila didn't really try to compete with the rest of the world. She'd never had the desire to. But seeing her wrap her arm around him like that made something explode inside her. "Aww, how sweet. She's still carrying a flame for you, love."

The woman blanched slightly and looked at her in confusion. "I'm sorry?"

"Well, Karter did tell me there were quite a few broken hearts in his past. I guess he just hadn't found what he was looking for yet." Lila tucked her hair behind her ears and reached out to grab his hand. "I guess we both got lucky."

Karter had a rueful smile on his face. He brought her hand to his lips and kissed it softly. "Yes, we did."

"Excuse me, I think I heard Sal calling. I'll be out with your food soon."

"It was lovely to meet you," Lila called after her. She tried to pull her hand away, but Karter refused. "Karter."

"Oh no, *love*. You gave me your hand, and I am not letting it go anytime soon."

Lila grumbled slightly. "I'm sorry. I don't know what came over me."

"I'm not, although chances are she might spit in our food."

"Let her. The little...." Lila snapped her mouth shut. She was not jealous. No, not a bit. What right did she have to be jealous? "Why are you grinning, Karter Knight?"

"Adam."

"What?" She blinked in confusion.

"You sounded like my mother there for a minute. All you

needed was the middle name," he teased her.

A blush filled her face and she tried to focus her thoughts, but Karter's finger was tracing lazy circles over the top of her hand, which made it really hard to think. "I have to go, Karter."

"You're not going anywhere, Lila." His voice was firm.

"Do you want me to pee on the floor?" She challenged him.

"Fine, but if I find you climbing out of the window there will be repercussions," he promised her.

Lila withdrew her hand and sucked in her breath. Part of her wondered exactly what he had in mind, but the rest of her was terrified to find out.

Sensing her anxiety, Karter chuckled softly. "I would never hurt you, Lila."

Wouldn't he, though? What he felt for her right now was the thrill of the chase. When he tired of it, Karter would toss her aside just like the waitress who was clearly still hung up over him. As she moved out of the booth a voice whispered across her mind.

Lila.

Her eyes flew to his and she gasped slightly. She moved away from the table and made her way to the bathroom at the back of the room. How could she hear him like that? His voice was as clear as day. It was a plea, from somewhere deep inside him. Lila did not understand the connection between them, only that it was there clear as day.

She refreshed herself in the bathroom and splashed water in her face. Sliding her back against the wall, Lila tried to get her thoughts together, but all she could think about was the way that one word seemed to echo between them. It was almost as if he were in pain. The idea that she could have been responsible for it made her want to heal it, no matter the personal cost.

Taking a deep breath, Lila made her way back to the table. She sat down across from him and looked down at the plate of food sitting in front of her.

"Everything all right?"

"No. Yes. I mean...." Lila took a drink of her water and tried to drown out the confusion that was running a marathon through her mind.

"Eat, Lila." His voice was soft and filled with concern. "You hardly touched any of your food last night."

She sighed in defeat and started to push her food around the plate. He was right. Her stomach was rather empty and seemed to rumble in protest. "You don't think she—"

"No, I already checked." He grinned at her. "You have nothing to worry about, Lila."

Lila snorted. "I have no claim over you, Karter."

His eyes turned golden for a moment, then back to their stormy blue. "Eat, Lila."

She looked down at her plate and started to eat the food in front of her. Lila was surprise how delicious it was. When she dropped syrup on her hand, she quickly licked it off before she could get sticky. She heard a fork drop on a plate next to her.

"Excuse me." Karter slid from the booth, making her wonder what was wrong.

Lila watched him walk away, and wondered why his body seemed so stiff when he was walking. Was he all right?

She was half-tempted to follow after him. Did he cut himself? Bite his tongue? She continued to imagine the worst when he did not return right away, but as much as she wanted to check on him, Lila was starving. She continued to eat her food, and had almost finished it by the time he returned.

When he slid across from her, he seemed to be a little calmer. Was that a look of relief when he saw her food was mostly gone? Lila had to be imagining that. "Are you okay?"

"I will be. Soon enough."

"Did I do something wrong?" Lila was starting to think she had.

Karter choked on his water. "No...you're fine."

She pushed her plate away from her and pulled some money out of her purse. "I really need to go, Karter."

"Put your money away, Lila." His hands covered hers.

"Why do you make me feel...?"

"What?" He asked her softly.

"Weak." Lila couldn't remember the last time she had cried so easily. Even when Grandma Tilly had passed, the tears had not come this close to the surface. Right now, she felt anything but strong.

"Maybe you've just been strong for too long?" he suggested.

Lila pulled her hands from his and pushed herself away from the table. She couldn't be near him like this. Every inch of her wanted to throw herself into his arms, but she could not give in to it. Everything she had built for herself would crumble and fall. As she left the diner, she couldn't help wondering what would be so wrong about that. She turned back to see the waitress smiling with her breasts yet again. That was precisely why she couldn't let herself fall for someone like Karter Knight.

Lila ran to her car and almost had it open before Karter walked through the door. His challenging stare told her that he would only follow her. So she did something unexpected—she squared her chin and walked over to him with a determination she wasn't quite sure resonated through the rest of her.

He stood there before her, waiting to see what she would do. When Lila reached out her hand to touch his face, she closed her eyes. His mouth kissed her palm and she sucked in her breath.

Her eyes flew open and saw the soft yearning in his eyes. "Why did you follow me?"

"Why did you run?" He challenged her.

"To protect you." She shivered slightly when the breeze blew across her face. As much as she felt the darkness, it seemed to be non-existent whenever he was around, and she couldn't quite understand why. "There's something I need to tell you."

"Me too. Trust me?" He offered his hand to her and Lila didn't have the heart to protest. He led her to his car, and she turned to look in the other direction.

"What about my car, Karter?"

"Damn it," he cursed. "Follow me?"

"Yes." To the ends of the earth, she wanted to add, but she closed her mouth before she could make the declaration. She went back to her car and put it into drive, determined to follow this through for the moment.

Chapter 9

Lila's heart was pounding in her throat as she followed Karter down a long gravel road. Where was he leading her to? And why was she chasing after him without asking? She sighed aloud. Clearly her mind was not in the right place, but she knew if she stopped following him right now, he would just turn around and come after her. Lila only had one choice, to see it through.

When the road started to thin a little, she realized that it wasn't a road, but a private drive. The closer they got, the more her intrigue grew. A two-story house with a beautifully landscaped front yard was at the end of the drive. She saw the garage door of the detached garage open and Karter drove his car inside it.

"What are you doing, Lila?" She had literally followed him to his wolf's den. Lila fought the urge to put her car in reverse.

Karter must have noticed her doubt. He walked over and smiled at her. "Come, Lila."

Every part of her brain screamed at her that this was not a good idea. If she walked inside that house, she was not going to return the same. Her heart would take over and the rest would be history. Karter's eyes met hers and she saw the loneliness inside, a loneliness she was sure he hid from the rest of the world. Turning the engine off, Lila smiled at him when he opened the door for her.

Lila put her hand on his cheek and kissed him softly on his lips. She wasn't sure why she did it, only that she wanted to. At first he didn't reply, but when his silky lips moved across hers she almost melted on the spot. When he broke the kiss, she sighed softly and put her head on his chest.

His hand stroked her back as he kissed the top of her head. "Come inside, Lila."

She hesitated for a second, but his eyes beckoned her as he held his hand out to her. Lila reached for it, loving the safe way she felt when his fingers slid over hers. When he opened the door for her, she wasn't sure what to expect. He was so flashy, so bright and dazzling. What she saw around her, though, was not the Karter she would have expected. In fact, a lot of what she saw there was familiar to her. Almost as if he had been building it for...no, that couldn't be. But when she saw the painting, she gasped. "I have that—"

"Painting?" he asked her curiously.

"Yes. I mean, it's much smaller and not nearly as beautiful. It's a replica."

"This is the original." Karter smiled at her.

"And this...." She touched one of the vases and closed her eyes. "How is this...?"

"I wish I had a good explanation. I've been building this

house for my mate."

"Mate?" Lila backed away slightly. What was he talking about?

"A man and his wolf can only have one mate. When we choose her, we will have no one else." Karter gestured for her to sit. "Please."

Lila sat down on the couch and crossed her legs. She wondered what on earth he was talking about, but was willing to hear him out, especially since it seemed so important to him.

"I've been...sowing my oats for long enough. My wolf is ready to settle down."

"And you?"

"I'm growing tired of the same old thing," Karter admitted.

"Oh." She still wasn't sure why he was telling her this, but the way he was looking at her made her feel slightly unnerved.

"I'm messing this up." Karter ran a hand through his hair. "What I'm trying to say is that I want...."

"Me?" squeaked Lila.

He gave her his most charming smile, and while that must have worked on all the other women in his life, Lila found it less than satisfactory. She glared at him and wanted to slap him across the face. Lila pushed up from the couch, her anger growing. How could he say those things to her? Had he lost his mind? Cruel and unusual punishment.

Suddenly she was desperate for some air. Lila looked for the nearest exit, but Karter anticipated her next move and stepped in front of her.

"Wait...hold on." He put his hand on her face. "I am not messing with you, Lila. I would never do that. I have never wanted anyone more than I do you. I've wanted you for longer than even I knew." Karter gestured to the house around him. "No one knows about this place. No other woman has ever been here. I take that back. My family knows about the house, but not why I built it."

"Why are you telling me this?" Lila shook her head and held her hand up.

"Because he doesn't want to talk, and I know if I did what he wanted, you'd run from me." Karter's eyes turned darker, and she saw the desire trickling across his face. He saw her shiver and his eyes softened. "I don't want you to be afraid of me, of him."

"I'm not afraid of either of you." Her chin rose proudly in the air and she bit the bottom of her lip, knowing full well it would drive him crazy. She put a hand out and pinched his arm.

"Ouch! What was that for."

"I wanted to make sure you were really here."

"Why?" he asked her quietly.

"Because the dream always ends before you get to the good stuff."

He sucked in his breath. "And just what do you see?"

Lila stepped closer and pulled his mouth down to hers. When he attempted to kiss her softly, Lila pulled him closer. His tongue slipped into her mouth and she closed her eyes. As he plundered deep inside her, she whimpered against him, which seemed to make him fumble for his control.

His lips slid down her face and she sighed in anticipation.

When he came closer to her neck, he pulled away and she wanted to scream at him. Every inch of her was filled with a crazy need she didn't understand, and all he had done was kiss her.

"I shouldn't do this — you need to know." His voice was hoarse as he tried to fight for control over himself. His eyes were almost bloodshot when he turned back to her.

"One mate for life?" she asked him.

"Yes...."

"I don't have many other options, Karter. It's not like I have men beating down my door, you know."

"I'd kill them." He growled and his eyes flashed angrily.

Lila giggled at the scene before her. Karter was literally plotting the death of fictional men who had never given her the time of day.

"It's not funny, Lila." His voice was sullen and just a tad bit grumpy.

"No...it's not." She looked down at the floor and shook her head. "The closest thing I've had to love is a man who haunts my dreams, Karter. I've never wanted anyone else. That man...he's you."

Karter let out a long breath of air. "Lila, this can't be undone. No second chances."

"Then you should know a few things, Karter. I — "

"I don't think you understand. No matter what you have to say to me, my wolf has chosen. He will never let me have another woman. Even if you decide to run away from me right here and now." He looked at the door, clearly afraid she would run. As if he had decided she would already leave, his eyes were filled with a great sadness and loss. "Please don't run."

"I don't want any of you to get hurt."

Karter sputtered slightly. "What are you talking about, Lila?"

"The reason I came here. I've been marked by something evil, something that wants to destroy me."

"Is that all?" He smiled softly at her.

"It's nothing to laugh at, Karter. It's real danger. This being, he's demonic." Lila pulled her shirt over her head and tossed it to the floor. Karter's eyes immediately fell over her white lace bra that barely concealed her flesh beneath. She rolled her eyes at him and turned around to let him look at the marks on her back.

"I'll kill it," he cursed.

"It's already dead...well, I'm not sure exactly how it exists, but it isn't from the living world. I was at the Vinson House, investigating with the TPRA." When she saw his confusion, she explained further. "Templar Paranormal Research Association. I'm a medium, Karter. I help them with some of their investigations."

"Like Brina." He grinned at her.

"She's a medium too?"

"Can't have too many of those in the family. So...you went to the Vinson house, and...."

"This thing...it was angry. It's keeping the spirits earthbound there. Draining the energy of the living near it. When I tried to leave, it attacked me. These wounds won't heal."

Karter reached down and kissed them with his lips, and Lila felt a soft tingling beneath his touch. His voice called to her. "Do you trust me?"

"Trust you...?" Lila wondered what he was going on about now, but she decided it was better to answer him to find out. "Yes."

She heard a whisper of movement behind her and felt teeth pull on her hand. Lila gasped and turned around. There was Karter in his wolf form. Lila reached her hand out to touch him, and smiled when his tongue snaked out to lick her hand. She giggled. "That tickles."

The wolf moved closer to her, and she wrapped her arms around his neck and hugged him tight. When he moved out of her arms, she pouted slightly. He raced around her and she felt his nose against her skin. His warm tongue licked her wounds, and at first she felt them burn just like they did any time she tried to clean them. Her spine tightened as she tried to keep herself from flinching. The more he licked her, the less it hurt, and she felt the warm hum of his healing balm flow through her. Lila sighed as she put her head on her knees, feeling at peace for the first time in weeks.

The next time she felt his breath on her back, it was in combination with Karter's soft lips as he trailed kisses up her spine. When his mouth reached her neck she sighed against him. His tongue snaked out to taste her, and she shivered with something she didn't quite understand.

He whispered into her ear, "I want to make you mine, Lila."

"How does it work?" She asked him softly.

"I have to bite you," he answered quietly.

She turned to face him. "Will it hurt?"

His hands traced her face. "It might. But less if I keep you distracted."

Lila searched his face. "Are you sure it's me, Karter? I would hate for you to—"

His mouth cut the rest of the words from her mouth as he scooped her up in his arms. He broke the kiss and lifted her into the air.

"What are you doing, Karter?"

"Making you mine, Lila. Before you try to talk me out of it again." He nuzzled her nose with his and she sighed against him.

"If you're sure."

"Yes, damn it. Now shut up, I'm going to kiss you," he warned her.

"But—"

His mouth was on hers before she could get another word out. Lila relaxed against him, realizing that real Karter was so much better than the dream one. As he started to carry her up the stairs, she could only guess at what was about to happen next. Unfortunately, the doorbell rang, breaking them from the reverie.

Karter broke their kiss, and was clearly fighting the fog of desire that was filtering inside him. He set her back on the floor and handed her shirt back to her that he had scooped up in his hand. She sighed in frustrated disappointment. Lila shoved the shirt over her head.

"Whoever it is, I'm going to kill them."

Lila was half considering homicide herself at the moment. She let out a ragged breath and tried to still the beat of her heart. Lila climbed the stairs that Karter was about to carry her up and looked for the closest bed to throw herself into.

It sounded like whoever was at the door was going to be awhile, and she did not feel like dealing with them. She closed her eyes and snuggled against one of the pillows on the bed, and smelled Karter's scent trapped within its fluffiness. Lila yawned and realized that she hadn't really slept last night. The moment she closed her eyes, she felt sleep calling to her.

Chapter 10

"What the hell are you doing here?" Karter shouted at Killian.

Killian looked over to the extra car in the drive. "Am I keeping you from something?"

Karter's eyes flashed furiously at his brother. "This better be good."

"There's been some trouble at the creek."

"Damn it. It's started again?" Karter ran a hand through his hair.

"Yes." Killian's face was pale. "The last time—"

"I know. It could have been Brina. Where is she?"

"Keeping an eye on Sophie. She's afraid to let her leave the house." Killian kicked the ground. "I thought he'd been banished."

"We'll take care of him, Killian. Just give me a minute."

"Of course. We need to search the grounds. There's another witch missing."

Karter growled. "I'll be right back."

Karter raced up the stairs to tell Lila that he had to go out, something he wasn't looking forward to doing when things were still unfinished between them. He walked into his room, and what he saw made his heart feel light. Lila was snuggled against his pillow, sleeping peacefully. He moved closer to the bed and ran his hand across her face. She sighed against it, and in that moment Karter knew he would do anything he could to protect the beautiful woman, an angel a man like himself did not deserve. Her innocence, her love, was the anchor that had been missing in his life.

Karter reached down and kissed her softly on the forehead, and pulled the covers closer to her chin. "I'll be back, Lila."

"*I love you...,*" she whispered in her sleep as a dreamy smile curved across her face.

Those words knocked the breath from his chest. He wanted more than anything to climb in beside her and snuggle her up against him, something he rarely did with any of the other women in his life. His playboy life, it had all come crashing to the shores the moment Lila had walked into his life.

Unfortunately, he had to leave her here like this. Karter cursed under his breath and his wolf growled inside him. It was time to go, and neither one of them was happy about it. Karter descended the stairs, grumbling the entire way. He found Killian sitting outside, leaning against the side of the house with his arms crossed lazily.

"You ready?" Karter growled at him.

"I almost feel sorry for you," teased Killian.

"Shut it," he sneered at Killian. "Let's get on with this."

Karter closed his eyes and let his wolf take over. He felt his skin start to recede as the fur quickly replaced it. His bones snapped and popped as he shifted into his beast form. Karter was now on autopilot, as Keelan, his wolf spirit, took over.

Keelan lifted his head into the air and howled almost as if he were in protest. The wolf paced outside the door of the house where his mate slept inside. Scratching at the ground, he sat back on his haunches and refused to move.

Killian grinned. "Come on, you. There's time for that later. You have to protect her now."

As if he understood his words, the wolf sprang to his feet. The drive to protect what was his would carry him faster than any other thing in this world. The world shifted fast before him as he sniffed out the woods around him. His brother raced ahead of him, and Keelan kept up with his flank. Another wolf came out of the woods and ran at his side. Keelan sniffed in his direction and grunted slightly. The wolf returned the gesture as they heard a howl a little further in the distance.

"ArooOOoooOO!"

A warning cry that something grizzly was up ahead. The wolf slowed its pace and stopped just on the outskirts of Witch's Hollow. He saw Killian pulling something down from a tree.

"Karter, help me."

The wolf released its form and returned control back over to Karter, who rose from the ground when he regained his humanity. "What the hell?"

"Where's her face?" Kam asked from behind him.

"Good of you to join us," Karter snorted. Karter couldn't remember the last time he'd seen his older brother. The last thing he had known, Kam had gone on what he called a walk-about, like he was in Australia or something. Karter didn't quite understand Kam. As the oldest, he should have been settled before now, but he kept to himself, refusing to take the chance to find his mate. Was he afraid of rejection or something?

Kam grunted at him. "I hear you have a mate."

"Soon."

Karter walked over to Killian and helped him bring the body down from the tree. He shivered when he saw the slashes that were deep across her face. Not because it was horrific, but because he recognized them. The same marks that had marred Lila's lovely skin. Had she brought it with her? Or was it the same evil that had always haunted the area?

"What did this?" Kam asked curiously.

"I'm not sure, but we need to put an end to it as soon as possible." Karter stood up and walked over to the nearest tree, and slammed his fist into it.

"What's up with him?" Kam nodded to Karter.

"He hasn't done the...."

"Oh...gotcha. Shame."

"How can you tease me at a moment like this?" Karter pointed to the body on the ground. "It's our job to keep this from happening."

"Sometimes there are things we cannot control." Kam shrugged his shoulders.

"And that would be why *you* aren't the alpha."

Kam growled at him, and was about to tear into him when Killian held his hand up. Killian's voice was sharp and grating. "Enough. You two act like you're on your cycle or something."

"Excuse me?" Karter eyed his brother with disdain.

"What was that?" Kam turned on him too.

"Shut the hell up, the both of you. We need to get this body to the witch's camp. They'll take care of her." Killian sighed in disgust. "Karter's right. We need to keep our eyes open. There was an older witch drowned at the creek, and now this one. That's two in one night. If it's starting again, it's making up for lost time."

Karter picked the woman up and slung her over his shoulder. "I'll get her there. You two keep searching."

Though the weight was more than he usually carried, Karter bore it with little complaint. Someone had loved her somewhere in this world. He treated her like precious cargo, knowing he would want someone to do the same if it were Lila. The very idea that this evil could be hunting her made every part of him inflamed. Karter would not rest until this thing was brought down.

As he traveled through the trees, Karter heard the snap of a twig. He heard a soft whimper and stopped to peruse the area. When his eyes settled on a small body, he lowered his load to the ground. Walking closer to the sound, he saw a little girl who was huddled on the ground. "Hello?"

The blue eyes looked up at him in fear and she scooted backward. "Don't hurt me."

"Whoa...whoa...hold on. I'm not going to hurt you." His thoughts turned back to the body on the ground, and he stepped back for a moment. He did not want the little girl to see the woman's face. Karter quickly took his shirt off and covered it.

"Are you lost?"

"Yes. My mother and I, we were...something horrible."

"What happened?" Karter crouched on the ground before her, fearing that the child might very well belong to the woman he was transporting back to the camp.

"We were following the moon. She was teaching me about the quarters, and then a dark shadow took her. I...I tried to find her. Her screams...." Tears filled the little girl's eyes. "I think she's...."

Karter had never felt so at a loss before. He'd dealt with loss, seen plenty of things that could turn a man's stomach. "I think...."

The child looked over to where Karter had come in and screamed. "Mama!"

Karter caught her mid run. "You can't."

"Mama!" Her tiny fists pummeled against him as she tried to break free from his grasp. She sobbed against his shoulder as Karter soothed her.

"It's going to be okay, little one. I'm trying to take her back to the witch camp." Karter didn't know what to do. She must have been five at the oldest, too young to see her mother in such a state. Karter heard a sound near him and sighed in relief.

"Kam...I need you to carry her." Karter scooped the child up in his arms and cradled her close to his body. "This child and her mother were out in the woods last night. She — "

Kam cleared his throat and nodded at him. "You go ahead. I'll bring this one."

"Sera," the child cried. "Her name is Sera."

Karter felt his eyes water as he thought about how he would feel if Sophie cried so pitifully. Maybe he was going soft, but his heart melted as the child put her head on his shoulder.

Her tears stained his skin and he held her tightly against him. He carried her as fast as his feet could manage, hoping that the child had someone who could help her through her grief. When he finally made it to the camp, several women had already gathered outside their huts.

"Sera!" One of them rushed over to the body. "Bring her inside here."

"It's not good," Kam warned her.

"Death never is. Where is Taela?"

"This one?" Karter answered softly. The child had fallen asleep in his arms as he carried her across the woods. "She was on her own. She heard her mother."

"Oh, good heavens! The poor thing."

"Does she have family?" Karter asked her.

"A grandmother somewhere. We can take her until we find her."

Karter tried to hand Taela over to her, but the child woke and started to scream. "No! No! No! Don't leave me."

Karter held his arms out helplessly in front of him as the child hung from his neck. He almost choked as she squeezed him tighter. The women tried to pry her off him, but she sobbed hysterically. He wrapped his arms around her and let her snuggle close to him. His heart melted when she stopped crying and quieted the moment he wrapped his arms around her.

"What are you going to do?" Kam asked him curiously.

Karter looked at him helplessly. He didn't understand it, but deep inside he knew that there was only one thing to do. He would have to take her home with him. "She can stay with me. Just until we figure out what to do."

Kam's eyes twinkled merrily. "You sure are —"

"Shut it." Karter glared at him.

"I was just going to say —"

"Kam." Karter fought the urge to growl at him. He didn't want to scare the child in his arms.

Killian whistled in surprise when he found the child attached to his brother. "A mate and a child. Did someone call for the apocalypse?"

"The world must be ending if *he* has a mate." Kam looked almost disgruntled.

"Not quite. He almost has a mate," teased Killian.

"I would *have* a mate if you hadn't barged in this morning."

"What's a mate?" Taela asked him.

The other men chuckled around him. He rolled his eyes at his brothers. "Glad to see you're amused."

The witch stepped closer and put her hand on Taela. "Taela, love. This is Karter. He's one of the Knights that protect the forest. He's got a lot of work to do. Why don't you come with me, child?"

"No, no, no, no, no. My knight." Taela's nails almost bit into his skin.

"She can come home with me. It's fine. I think Lila will be able to help with her."

At least he hoped she would. Karter knew very little about how to help a child. He got on just fine with Sophie, but truth be known, that was only because he let her do pretty much what she wanted to, which only ended up getting him in trouble with Brina. What in the world was he going to do? And as much as he wanted to protect this child, he also needed to make his mark before Lila decided to run from him.

He still didn't know how he was going to explain this to her.

Chapter 11

Lila yawned and stretched as she wiped the sleep from her eyes. How long had she been asleep? She looked over at the alarm clock and found it was seven in the evening. What in the world? Had she been that tired? Climbing out of the bed, she wondered where Karter was.

Lila walked down the stairs and was surprised that Karter was nowhere to be found. Her first thought was that he had changed his mind. Had she done something wrong? Her instinct to run was deeply ingrained in her—why, she didn't know. It had always been there every time she had raced away from him in her dreams. Not this time though. She was going to stay put, to find out where she stood once and for all.

Lila opened the front door and went to retrieve her things. First, she needed her bag from the front seat. The moment she opened her door, she heard Karter's voice.

"Don't go, Lila." There was fear in that plea.

Lila turned around to see him coming out the front

door. His face looked defeated, as if something horrible had happened. "Karter...I didn't...."

"You're running, aren't you?" His eyes were tortured.

Lila shook her head and walked over to him. She touched her hand to his face. "I'm not."

His eyes told her he did not believe her. She smiled at him and brought his face down for a kiss, but he pulled away. Lila stepped back and tried not to read too much into that one action. Something had changed. Earlier, he had been ready to devour her inch by inch. Now...he was retreating.

"Should I go?"

"No! Damn it. I—"

A loud scream erupted from the house and Karter raced inside. Lila wondered what in the world was going on, and while her emotions were still reeling, she followed after him. What she saw nearly took her breath away. A small child was clinging to him for dear life. When her eyes looked up at Lila she sucked in her breath. Blue. Almost as vivid as Karter's. Was this...?

"Um, I...."

"I just have to get her back to sleep, Lila. Then we can talk."

The way his hands gently soothed the child told her all she needed to know. The child was hurting. Whether she was some hidden love child or not, she needed comfort. Lila closed the door behind her and walked closer to the pair of them. As Lila reached her hand out to the child, Karter pulled her away. Lila flinched slightly. Was she not good enough to touch her? She closed her eyes and tried to hide the pain that ripped through her.

A tear fell down her face, and she opened her eyes to find the child clinging onto him for dear life. "I think I should go."

Lila. He called out to her, one plea that kept her frozen to her spot.

"I want my mama!" the girl cried pitifully.

The cry tore her heart to pieces. She understood the feeling. Lila wanted someone desperately too. Lila took a deep breath and promised herself that she was going to weather this storm no matter how many bumps and bruises she got along the way.

She ignored Karter's warning and put her hand on the girl. "Hello, there. I'm Lila."

The girl stopped crying and turned to look at her with a sorrow that broke her heart. Something tragic had happened to this girl. A whisper ran across her mind. *Please help her.*

Lila turned to the sound of a young woman, who was filled with great sorrow. "Excuse me." Lila walked away from them and closed her eyes. *Who are you?"*

Sera. He's coming for her.

Lila shivered at the warning. *Show me.*

Lila held her hand up and felt the spirit touch her hand. The image of a dark shadow slammed into her. Lila saw the shadow hissing and spitting as it chased after the mother and her child. The witch cast a shield protecting her child as she led the demon through the forest far away from her child. Lila saw the burst of angry red light as it slashed against her face. The demon siphoned her light away, one drop at a time, before the witch was drained of her life completely. She had not been the only target. Lila gasped and turned around to look at the child, who was crying in Karter's lap.

Keep Taela safe.

Lila nodded at the white glowing light that was fading quickly. *I will.*

He's calling me. I can't fight him much longer.

A tear fell down Lila's face as she realized how Karter had found this child. She wasn't his, not like she had assumed at first. Lila walked to the door and heard Karter's voice.

"Lila, please don't."

She didn't answer him. Not because she was leaving, but because her words would have been filled with such sorrow. She didn't have the energy to explain what she was doing. Heading out to the car, she looked under her driver's seat to retrieve the one thing that she knew would protect her. Then she opened the trunk and dug around in her luggage to retrieve the last thing she had from Grandma Tilly. The tiny disheveled bear had been well loved. The first stuffed animal Lila had ever had. He had always made her feel safe when the entire world seemed against her.

When she opened the door, she saw the torture on Karter's face and offered him a soft smile of encouragement. Lila knelt down next to the child. "Taela, you need to give Karter a break. You're going to drown him with your tears, love."

The little girl sniffed and pouted as she turned to look at her. "I want my mama."

"I know, love. Come here." Lila offered her arms to the child, who looked from Karter to the stuffed dog in Lila's hands. When she climbed into Lila's arms, she carried her off to the kitchen with Karter watching her with surprise.

"Taela, you must be hungry. Tell me what Sera made for you."

"You know my mother?"

"She's a beautiful woman who will be with you always." Lila touched the child's heart. "Right here and here."

The child put her hand on her head. "Like Tilly?"

Lila was caught off guard for a moment. "You know about Tilly?"

"I'm sorry, was I not supposed to say that?" The child's lips wobbled.

Lila tapped her on the nose with her finger. "You can tell me anything you want, Taela."

She set the child on the kitchen counter, and when she looked like she was going to start crying again, she looked at her seriously. "This is Keelo...he gets scared sometimes. Can you keep him safe?"

"Yes." Taela held the dog tight.

"Ah-ah. Not too tight, love, or you'll hug the stuffing out of him." Lila turned to the refrigerator and looked through its contents. "Well, look here." Lila pulled out an apple and handed it to her. "That's a good start. Now, if Karter can just tell me where the peanut butter is, I make an amazing peanut butter sandwich."

Karter leapt from the couch, still entranced by the way she had taken charge of the situation. He rifled through the cabinets and pulled out a jar of peanut butter, then found her a loaf of bread. "Anything else?"

"A glass of milk, I think. Right, Taela?"

"Yes, please." The child had the largest lips that pouted without even trying.

Lila rubbed the top of her head before kissing it. "It will be all right."

"That's what Tilly says."

"And Grandma Tilly is always right, love." She felt her grandmother's love surrounding her, and for once it didn't bring the tears that usually accompanied it. It was almost as if Tilly had brought her here. Which was pretty unbelievable, really, but stranger things had happened. Like mysterious dreams that led her to the remarkable man who was standing before her.

"Now here is the question of the hour—strawberry or grape?" Lila asked Taela.

"Grape." She smiled softly at Lila.

"Grape it is." Lila quickly made the sandwich and put it on the plate that Karter had put on the counter. She carried the plate to the kitchen table, then turned around to scoop Taela off the counter. "Come on, love, let's get some food in that belly."

Lila sat the child down on the chair and started to walk away, but the child latched her arms onto her. Lila sighed and turned around to face her. Lila saw the fear in her eyes and it ate at her soul. She reached inside her pocket and retrieved the pentacle that Amber Knight had given her. "Do you see this?"

"Yes." The girl nodded at her.

"A powerful witch gave me this to protect me. She's just as strong as your mama, who protected you last night. I want you to have it." Lila slid the necklace over the child's neck and kissed her on top of her forehead. "It will keep you safe. I promise."

"Witch's honor?" Taela whispered.

"Witch's honor." Lila held up her hand in a solemn swear.

"I'll be right back, Taela."

Lila walked into the hallway and the tears started to fall down her face. That thing had attacked this poor child, she knew it. Had Lila brought it here? Guilt ate at her soul and she tried to keep calm, but the minute Karter whispered her name, she threw herself into his arms.

"Shh...." He cradled her against him. His hands rubbed her back as she sobbed quietly into his shoulder.

"It's my fault...I should never have come here." Lila tried to push away from him, but he refused to let her go.

"You are *not* running away, Lila." His voice was almost a growl.

"Look what happened!" Lila nodded to the child in the other room.

"This was not your fault. And it is not the first time that thing has attacked Witch's Hollow."

A chill ran up her back. "What?"

"It's been four years since the last attack. We thought he'd been banished."

Lila shuddered, afraid to believe him. When she looked up at him, she saw he was speaking the truth. "How is that possible?"

"Dark magic? Some things never make sense. All I know is right now, there is a child in that room who is scarred for life. Her mother...."

"Sera."

"How in the world did you know all that?"

She narrowed her eyes on him. "Really?"

"Oh...right. Medium." He grinned ruefully.

"Good enough to learn that this thing has Sera trapped

within its clutches. He feeds on white light, Karter. And Sera wasn't his target."

"Taela?" Anger flashed in his eyes, and she knew that Karter and his wolf were now in defensive mode.

There was still a part of her that wondered if he was Taela's father, but even so, she couldn't believe he would desert his child. If he had one. "She'll be fine. Your mother's magic is strong."

"That magic was meant for you, Lila," he reminded her.

"I'm fine." Lila went to kiss him on the cheek, and he turned his mouth at the last second. She sighed beneath his lips, more than ready to lose herself to his magical touch, but the sounds of a child crying out for her broke through the bliss.

Karter stiffened next to her when Lila broke the kiss. He tried to pull her closer, but Lila evaded him. She walked into the other room and kept her emotions under lock and key.

"What's wrong, ladybug?" Lila asked her.

"I spilled my milk." Her mouth wobbled as she pointed to the mess on the floor.

"Uh-oh. I guess we'll have to clean that up, huh?" Lila winked at her. "Do you want to help?"

"Yes." The child hopped out of the chair and took Lila's hand.

"Let's see...ah. Here's some towels." Lila pulled some dish towels out of a drawer and handed one to Taela. The two of them cleaned up the milk in a matter of seconds.

"Are you full?"

"Yes." The child's eyes seemed to be fighting gravity.

"Come here, love. Let's find somewhere to get some

sleep."

Karter cleared his throat behind her. "I have a room down here."

"Perfect." Lila scooped the child up in her arms. "Bring me a shirt, will you?"

Lila carried Taela into the room and saw the bathroom inside. "Oh...look at that. Let's take a small potty break, shall we?"

Taela followed her into the bathroom and Lila nodded to the toilet. "I'll just be right outside this door, okay?"

"Okay."

When she walked out of the door, Karter came into the room with a shirt and a spare toothbrush and toothpaste. She couldn't help thinking how sexy he was, and all he was doing was something a father might do for a child. When he stepped closer to her, his eyes flashed the same golden light that took her breath away.

He stopped before her and whispered in her ear, "If you keep looking at me like that, I'm liable to take you right here on this floor."

She blinked in confusion and took the things he handed to her. His breath was still at her throat, and she shivered as she thought about him doing just that. His mouth kissed her neck and she sighed aloud. Her entire body felt as if every nerve ending was screaming for his touch.

"Lila?" the small voice called out to her.

Karter growled and pulled away from her. "I'm going to go take a shower."

"I'm here, Taela. Are you finished?"

"Yes."

Lila pushed the door open and smiled at the little girl. "I have a shirt you can sleep in."

"Thank you."

Lila quickly helped the girl change and brush her teeth. By the time they were done, it was clear that Taela was beyond exhausted. "Come, let's get you to bed."

Lila led her to the bed, and smiled when she found the girl carrying the stuffed dog with her. She wrapped the covers around Taela and held her close to her body until the child fell asleep. Only when she could move without disturbing her did Lila pull herself out of the bed.

Chapter 12

When Lila closed the door behind her, she almost gasped in surprise. Karter was waiting right outside the door. She held up a finger to her mouth and nodded for him to move away from the door. It was now closer to nine. The last time she'd eaten was yesterday morning.

As she moved into the living room she felt his breath at the back of her neck. His arms wrapped around her stomach and pulled her tight against him. She sighed against him as his hands caressed her belly. His lips were warm on her skin as he teased her neck lightly. Lila leaned against him, ready to sink into the pleasure only he could teach her. When he released her, she pouted.

"I made you some food."

She turned to smile at him. "You're very thoughtful."

"You're going to need your energy, Lila."

"So, you've ulterior motives?" she teased him.

His eyebrows rose and he gave her a sexy grin. "Always."

Lila giggled. "I see."

Lila made her way into the kitchen and found two plates filled with sandwiches, just like the one she had made for Taela. He had sliced an apple and set a few bags of chips on the table. Two candlesticks were glowing in the darkness. Lila wasn't sure whether to be charmed or demand a real meal, but the smile on his face showed that he knew how pitiful his meal was.

Lila smiled at him. "Didn't have time to go shopping this week?"

"How did you know?"

"We're more alike than you know." She gave him a knowing smile. When he pulled her chair out for her Lila giggled softly. "Is this a date?"

"I think we're well past the dating stage." His eyes roamed over her face and moved down to the chest that she had unwittingly exposed earlier.

Lila felt a heated blush fill her face. "It would seem so."

Lila ate her food quietly, and marveled at how delicious the sandwich tasted. He used more peanut butter than she did, probably because Lila was afraid to use too much at once. Her budget didn't have a lot of wiggle room. Speaking of which, she'd really have to find some time to work tomorrow if she wanted to pay the bills. She had not intended to sleep away the day. Then again, there were a lot of things she had never intended. She seemed to be throwing the handbook out the window these days.

Lila saw him watching her eat. "What are you thinking about?"

"You don't want to know." He had barely touched his food.

"Karter?" She was starting to worry about him. "Are you okay?"

"I will be. Are you done?"

Lila blinked in confusion and then looked down at her plate. She had cleaned the whole thing, every last crumb. "Yes."

She rose to take her plate to the sink, but nearly jumped when his voice bit out. "Leave it."

"But—"

"Upstairs...now." A golden light erupted across his eyes as Karter tried to rein himself in.

"I—"

"Lila, if you don't go upstairs, you may find yourself bent over the back of this table."

"Oh...." She bit her bottom lip and saw his muscles tense slightly. Lila couldn't help wondering what that might actually be like, but the way his mouth ticked told her that now was not the time to be considering such things.

"Karter...," she called back to him as she started to leave the kitchen.

"Yes?"

"Can you bring my bags upstairs?"

He schooled his face and nodded toward the upstairs. "I'll be up in a little while, Lila."

When she headed up the stairs, she heard him berating himself and fought the urge to giggle. He really was struggling with this. And while she was curious about what would happen next, she wasn't in near the turmoil he was. She almost felt sorry for him.

Lila heard him leave the house and return within a few

minutes. She waited for him to climb the stairs, but she heard Taela call out his name. The next thing she heard was Karter's soft voice singing a lullaby to the child, who was still terrified from the night before. The fact that he could control his wolf long enough to comfort someone who really needed him made another part of her shell crash to the ground. Karter may not even realize the kind of man he was — noble, brave, and heaven help her, the most attractive man she had ever laid her eyes on.

Sighing softly, she walked downstairs to retrieve her bag. The door was open and she saw he was snuggling the child in his lap. Their eyes met, and she smiled softly at him before closing the door to give them more privacy.

As she made her way up to the bedroom, she heard him whisper across her mind. *I'll be up soon.*

She shivered in anticipation.

When she made it up to the room, she went through her bag trying to find something that was even remotely sexy. One nightgown after another...not anything to make a man's blood pressure boil. She sighed in defeat. Flannel nightgown it was. At least it didn't go all the way up to her chin and only went down just beyond her knees. It really just looked like an oversize man's flannel shirt. Lila liked to be warm when she slept, and these always seemed to do the trick. When she didn't have any romantic inclinations, being practical had been cost effective and apparently boring as hell. There was nothing she could do about it. She wasn't about to spread herself naked on his bed.

Lila walked over to the armchair near the window. She sat down and looked outside. The moon cast a haunting glow on the world below. Lila could see the outline of the trees outside. The forest surrounded his property in pretty much every direction. It was beautiful. The more she waited, the harder it was to keep her eyes open. She had no idea how late it was when her eyes closed.

Lila was in another haunting dream, chased by the wolf that wanted to make her his. Tackled by both, Lila looked up into his burning eyes and shivered. The desire inside was so hard that she almost feared his touch. Her dream lover brought his lips down to hers and she shivered in anticipation. His mouth barely touched hers before moving down to her neck, down to the valley of her breasts, and just when she thought the dream would stop, she found herself floating on air.

"*Please don't stop...,*" she whispered aloud.

"For the love of...," Karter's voice growled.

Her eyes snapped open and she gasped at the sheer anger on his face. "Karter?"

"If I can't have you, there's no way in hell I'm letting some dream take over." Karter's eyes flashed and he crept closer.

Lila nibbled on her bottom lip and heard the growl that resonated deep in his chest. The blues of his eyes seemed to disappear, and Lila realized his wolf was being pushed past its limit. The wild animal beneath the surface was fighting for control of his body.

Lila held out her hand to him. "I'm not afraid."

"I am...," he whispered. "I don't want to hurt you."

Lila sat up and met him halfway on the bed. "Kiss me."

Karter flinched. "He doesn't...we don't want just — "

"Good, because I'd like to finish my dream. There's quite a few pieces you keep forgetting to fill in."

His mouth devoured hers, the heat and intensity almost taking her breath away. The buttons of her gown seemed to annoy him as his hands tried to open them. She heard the rip of fabric as the gown was torn from her body. He broke the kiss. "Scared yet?"

Lila rubbed her nose against his. "Never."

Karter groaned as his mouth ran a path of fire down her face. When he stopped at her throat, Lila knew he was trying to control himself, but she felt the need in every inch of his taut body. He wanted to bite her.

Lila reached up and pulled him down onto her. "Do it, Karter."

He growled as his teeth suck into her flesh. There was pleasure in the pain as she arched off the bed. She whimpered as parts of her body were now clearly waking up. Lila wanted more—she needed him to finish what he'd started.

He licked her wound and drew back slightly. His voice was tortured when he saw the raw flesh under him. "I hurt you."

Lila wanted to hit him. If he stopped now, she was going to physically maim him. She pushed up from the bed and launched herself at him. Her breasts slid against his chest as her mouth reached out for his. She caught him by surprise as he brought her against him. Her hands wrapped around his neck and pulled him as close as humanly possible. Lila did not know what she wanted. She had never been here before, but a need greater than the air she breathed ripped through her.

He broke the kiss when a cry erupted from downstairs. "Son of a—"

Lila felt a tear slide down her cheek. Not again. She felt the need inside him. It was greater than her own. Lila pulled him closer to her and wrapped her legs around him. "You have to finish it, Karter."

The gold light took over him and he pushed himself deep inside her. Lila winced as he stretched himself past her virginal wall. She didn't care. Wrapping her legs around him, she refused to let him withdraw. As he moved, a heat began to build inside her, something delicious that was kindling at a lower pitch. She might not find the fantasy she craved right now, but she was pretty sure Karter would make it up to her later. Her hands roamed over his back and her insides bunched as she felt his excitement climb. When his whole body went tight, she felt him plunge inside her one last time. A warm heat filled her core, and she realized that Karter had found his finish. In good time, too, for Taela's screams started to get louder.

He pushed away from her and pulled his jeans back on. Lila wasn't even sure when he had lost them. She saw the regret on his face and she waved him off. "Go. She needs you."

When she moved on the bed, she saw there was blood on the comforter. She got up from the bed and went into the bathroom to find something to clean herself off with. Closing the door behind her, she sank against the door and slid to the floor. She wasn't upset that he had taken her virginity, only that it had not been the dream she had seen in her head so many times. Had it been horrible? No, but it hadn't exactly been spectacular either. She knew he would have waited, but she had pressed him, so Lila was just as responsible for this as he was. It had been the right call, as much as she hated to admit it. The wolf would only have driven Karter crazy until he had his way.

Lila stood up and walked into the other room. She found one of Karter's T-shirts in one of the dressers. She put it on and went into the master closet to see if there was another comforter inside. She was not disappointed. Pulling it off the shelf, she found the other linens to change the bed so it matched.

Chapter 13

Lila had just finished changing the bedding. Now she was in the bathroom, trying to scrub her blood from the beautiful quilt. She almost jumped when Karter poked his head through the door.

"What are you doing, Lila?"

"I...."

He glanced down at the stain and cursed inwardly. "I hurt you."

"No...." She held up her hand to try to ease his concern.

"You're bleeding."

"No...I was bleeding." She blushed. "It's kind of what happens sometimes when you're...."

"Damn it." Karter ran his hands through his hair. "I didn't mean for it to go like that, Lila."

"It's okay, Karter—" She tried to cram all her emotions deep inside. It hadn't gone the way she wanted either, but she didn't want him to punish himself. There was no point in that.

"I called my mother," Karter interrupted her.

"I'm sorry...why would you do that?" Lila's face turned red hot.

"Not about that...I wanted to know how to get her to sleep." He grinned boyishly at her. "If I told her about the way I manhandled you, I wouldn't have any parts to ever do it again."

"That would be a loss," she whispered.

He shuddered. "I gave her some warm milk and some melatonin. She should be out like a light."

"Oh, okay." Lila kept scrubbing at the stains. She was afraid to look up at him.

"Lila...."

"Yes, Karter?"

"Damn it, forget the comforter. Come here."

"But it's so pretty...." She looked up at him and her breath caught in her throat. His eyes were filled with the same heat as before. He couldn't possibly be planning...or was he?

Karter walked over to her and pulled the comforter from her hands. "I'll buy you three more, but if you don't come to bed, so help me, I will drag you there myself."

Lila gasped, and knew from the hard set of his chin that Karter meant business. She walked quietly from the bathroom and turned to find him on her heels. Lila almost squeaked aloud.

Karter's mouth came down to hers, and when she thought he would pillage its depths, the caress was soft and sweet. When his tongue slid inside she sighed against him. His hand slid under the shirt and found its way to one of her breasts. When he ran his thumb over her nipple Lila gasped, giving him the perfect opportunity to slide his tongue further into her mouth.

Karter broke the kiss long enough to slide the shirt slowly up her stomach. The material caressed her skin as he moved it over her breasts. When he tossed it on the floor, Lila realized she was naked before him for the second time that night. He held her at arm's length and took in every inch of her flesh with his eyes.

Lila looked down at the ground, afraid to see disappointment anywhere on his face. Her fingers strummed the top of her lip and her breath caught in her chest.

"God, you're beautiful."

Her eyes shot up to his to see what cruel trick he was playing on her. No man had ever called her that before. Of course, none of them had ever gotten this close to her before. He was completely entranced with her, and for once, she saw herself in a different light and it scared the hell out of her. "What if Taela...?"

"She's going to sleep, Lila."

"Are you sure you don't want to...?" Lila was suddenly afraid of what was about to happen next. What if she didn't really please him?

"Time to stop talking, Lila." His eyes were filled with a desire that shook her to the core.

"If you—"

His mouth covered hers, swallowing any last words. As he did, Karter walked her slowly to the bed. He stopped only long enough to yank the comforter off the bed. When he turned to look at her, he found the doubts inside her mind, but misinterpreted them. "I'm usually much better at this,

Lila. I promise by the time I'm done, you won't remember it."

She shivered as he crept closer to her. Lila fell back against the bed and found herself staring up at him. She watched him remove his shirt, and admired his muscled chest. His pants followed, and she was shocked to find that he was still very much aroused. "How...?"

"When a man and his wolf align, anything is possible." He crawled into bed over her and kissed her softly. "It also helps to have a naked woman ready and willing. You are willing, right?"

She shivered against him. "Yes, please."

"Good. I think I might die if you refuse me," he whispered into her ear. His tongue reached out behind her lobe and licked her spot. "That one freckle...I swear it haunts me."

"What are you...? Oh...."

She moaned when he took her ear lobe into his mouth and nibbled it slightly. His hand was rubbing against her nipple. The friction was delicious. His mouth moved away from her ear and worked its way down her neck. As he did, his hands parted her legs. The moment his mouth took her nipple inside it, his finger tweaked against her clit. The breath caught in her throat. A jolt of electricity shot through her as he suckled against her. His finger set a gentle pace that caught her off guard. Lila was unable to keep a single thought in her head. All she could think about was the swirling heat that started to form in her womb.

Her breath came in short gasps as something built inside her. What was he doing to her? She felt a heat rush through her as her body reached out to something completely foreign to her.

He released her breasts and kissed her stomach softly. "Come on, Lilah. That's it, baby. Let go for me."

Lila whimpered when he kissed her stomach. His fingers moved faster and she felt a frenzy take over her. She wanted something she couldn't name, and her body sped toward it. When the tight spring inside her uncoiled, her legs started to shake. A ripple of pleasure raced through her. Karter growled as he bit her nipple.

She moaned as his fingers continued to work her over. She just wanted to curl up in a delicious ball and take in the pleasure he had released in her, but Karter pushed her forward to something even more spectacular. Arching into his mouth, she reveled in the way her desire pushed him further.

He pulled away from her and she whimpered in protest. Karter kissed her pouting lips. "You're so wet for me, Lila."

Lila pulled him down to her, and shuddered against his heat. Their naked bodies together were almost too much for her to bear, especially with his magical touch sending her over the edge again. When she started to moan loudly, he cut her cries off with his mouth. His tongue plundered inside her mouth and his hips ground into hers, mimicking the motion she craved more than anything else. She rocked against his fingers, desperate to find herself in his touch.

When he broke away from her kiss, she pleaded with him. "Please...."

"Not yet, Lila." He pulled away from her and withdrew his hands from her clit. "You look so disappointed."

A tear fell down her face, and Lila hadn't realized she was crying. Karter kissed it away. His eyes were filled with emotion too. His nose rubbed against hers and she sighed.

He pulled her up from the bed and cradled her in his arms. Karter ran a hand down her spine as he kissed her softly on the lips. He moved her so her back was facing him. His mouth trailed gentle kisses down her back, kisses that took her breath away. When his fingers tweaked against her nipples, she whimpered softly. He kept it up until Lila thought she would lose her mind.

Pulling her tight against his chest, his fingers sought entrance to her core and she felt him slide them inside her. His other hand swept around to rub against her clit.

"Ohhh...," she whimpered as her body took over for her. Her hips ground against him as she took her fill of him, but his hands weren't what she really wanted. He refused to give her that yet. Lila had to be satisfied with the pleasure he was offering her for the moment. Soon, she was fighting back the orgasm that threatened to wipe sanity from her brain. When his teeth bit into her shoulder, she lost all hope of controlling herself. She felt herself shatter around his talented fingers.

"You're dripping." She shuddered against him. "I want to sink into you so badly."

Lila came hard against him again as she imagined him deep inside her. Her body craved that more than life itself. "Please...."

Karter almost pushed her off his lap. She turned around and looked up at him. Lila saw the control he was fighting to maintain. His duality was clearly clashing with itself.

She reached for his hand. "I want you — *all* of you, Karter."

He groaned as he let go of his reservations. Karter slid her legs open and rested his cock just outside her wet core. First he slid gently inside, teasing her with his tip. Lila was almost mad with desire by the time he slid into her. There was only a small remnant of soreness left inside her. The only ache she had was for him to take her along with him one last time. As he moved in and out of her, she closed her eyes and enjoyed the slow sensual rhythm that he set as he led her over the mountain. When she made it over to the edge, she let her body fall into the abyss. She soared over the world in a cloud of desire that would have brought the strongest person to her knees. When he joined her, she almost shouted with joy.

As their breathing started to settle, Lila felt him still warm inside her. She quivered around him and his cock seemed to twitch. He moved it deeper inside her and she lost all will to breathe. "Oh...."

"You drive me crazy, Lila," he whispered in her ear.

"Mmmm....the feeling is mutual." She felt her eyes growing heavy as a sleepy coma threatened her. Lila yawned and stretched, and found that only made her draw him into her even further. Her breath caught in her throat as she tensed around him.

His mouth came down to her face. He ran small butterfly kisses over her eyelids before he nuzzled her with his nose. The sound of a crying child interrupted their moment, and Lila tried to push him up.

Pulling out of her, he whispered, "Sleep, Lila. I'll stay with her."

Lila's eyes drifted shut and she snuggled deep under the covers that he pushed over her. She sighed in contentment as the warmth surrounded her. For once, she knew if she dreamt about the dream lover tonight, she could fill in all the blanks from reality.

Chapter 14

Lila gasped for breath and her hands clawed for any sense of life. She felt strong arms grab her hands. Shrieking, she fought tooth and nail to try to break free.

"Lila! Wake up!" Karter's voice shouted at her.

Her eyes snapped open and she started to sob uncontrollably. Karter wrapped his arms around her and held her tight against him. Lila was gasping for air, trying to unsee the horrors that echoed inside her mind. When Karter tried to pull away from her, she pulled him closer.

"Don't leave me," she begged him.

He kissed the tears that ran down her face. "I'm here, Lila."

For how long, though? The dream had been so real. Her throat still hurt, the hands had squeezed so tight. She tried to swallow and ended up coughing. Lila loosened her grip and ran a finger across her throat. Her skin was raw to the touch.

Karter glanced down at her neck. "What the hell!"

Lila pushed up from the bed and raced to the bathroom.

She looked in the mirror and saw several raw gashes were circling her throat. They looked a lot like the scratches that had appeared on her back.

Karter came into the bathroom behind her, his eyes boiling with anger. "Did I do that?"

"What?" she asked in confusion.

"I bit you." Suddenly he looked very troubled.

"No!" She reached for his hands. "This isn't you."

"Then how did that get there? If he did this to you, I just...." Karter pulled away from her and slammed his fist into the wall.

"Karter...neither one of you did this. My dream...." Lila wasn't sure how she was going to explain it to him. It really didn't make sense to herself. Lila turned around and looked at her back. What she saw made her gasp aloud. "Karter!"

"Now what!" His eyes searched hers.

"You healed them." The scratches on her back were only a small pink trail compared to what they had been.

He reached out and ran his fingers over the pink lines, and Lila shivered under his touch. "Does that hurt?"

"No," she whispered. Not unless he stopped. Unfortunately, Lila could see the morning light starting to trickle through the window. As much as her thoughts were turning to something else entirely, she was sure that Taela would be up soon.

As if he had just realized that Lila was standing naked before him, the angry flash in his eyes disappeared. Something else was waking up entirely. Karter's mouth kissed her shoulder blade as his arms wrapped around her. His hands roamed up her stomach, his gentle strokes making her clench her stomach. When his fingers stroked over her nipples, she sucked in her breath.

"Karter...what about Taela?"

"She's gone," he answered between kisses as his lips caressed her skin.

"What do you mean, she's gone?" Lila pulled away from him, panic filling her.

"Relax, Lila. Her grandmother came for her." He smiled ruefully.

"Why didn't you wake me up?" Lila shook her head at him.

"You were sleeping so peacefully." His fingers stroked the marks around her throat. "Now I wish I would have. Are you going to tell me about these?"

"Not yet. I believe you were telling me how we're completely alone in this house." Lila moved closer to him and slid her hands under his shirt. She felt his skin ripple under her touch.

He cleared his throat when her hands slid up further. "Yes...alone."

Her fingers tweaked over his nipples and he captured her mouth with his. The hunger behind his kiss was just starting to grow. Lila enjoyed the way he reacted to her touch. It made her feel like she had some power over him. She slid her hand down his stomach and he almost jumped back from her.

"What are you doing, Lila?"

She nibbled the bottom of her lip. "Did I do something wrong, Karter?"

"No."

"Good." She moved closer to him again and let her

hand slide under the band of his sweats, and reveled in the knowledge that it was the only barrier to his flesh below. When her fingers brushed against the tip of his erection, she licked the bottom of her lip before biting it with her teeth.

Karter jerked against her. His eyes had taken on a dangerous glow. "If I hadn't seen it with my own eyes, I would be seriously doubting your virginal state right now."

"You've corrupted me, Karter Knight." She pouted and withdrew her hand. "But if you're not interested, I guess I can—"

Before she knew it, Lila found herself almost flying through the air as Karter flung her over his shoulder. She shrieked. "What are you doing?"

"Making sure you always remember who you belong to." He tossed her on the bed and she giggled at him. "You think I'm kidding." His eyebrow rose sardonically as he crept closer to her, losing one article of clothing with each step.

Lila gasped when he slid her legs apart. "What are you...? Oh...."

Karter's tongue shot out to lick the most intimate part of her body. Silky soft strokes against her clit made her stomach contract painfully. Sparks ignited inside her, and she moaned in surprise. A languid fire was building inside her, and Lila was enjoying every minute of it. Her legs shook when he brought her first orgasm to life. As he did, he nibbled on her clit before sucking her hard into his mouth.

Lila's hands gripped the sheets and she moaned for more. "Karter."

His growl caught her off guard before he lapped at the juices pooling between her legs. He bit the inside of her thigh and licked her skin. "Every inch just as sweet as the rest."

She sighed when his mouth returned to her clit. This time when he sensed her getting closer, he withdrew. Lila whimpered softly, craving the finish he denied her.

"Poor sweet, Lila. Were you close? Good." His teeth bit her leg again before his mouth swooped back to torture her some more.

Her core was throbbing painfully when he brought her finish so close but just out of reach. A frenzy was building inside her, and all she wanted was to feel him slide his warmth inside her. Lila didn't know how to ask him to put her out of her misery, and wasn't even sure he would be all that inclined to do so. He was enjoying her condition, for every time she got closer, he would draw himself away.

Lila did not understand why he was dragging it out. Why didn't he just put her out of her misery? His tongue teased her again, and this time when she was ready to finish, she reached down and wrapped her hands in his hair and held him in place. He growled against her, lapping at her like a hungry beast as she came hard against him. The painful pleasure that ripped through her had her screaming his name. "Karter!"

Her hands released him and he climbed up her slowly, kissing and biting her along the way. When his mouth covered hers, she drank him in. Their tastes mingled together like a sweet spice as their tongues tried to master each other. Karter broke the kiss and went back to his favorite spot behind her ear. His tongue snaked out to lick it before he whispered, "That craziness you feel, that need — it consumes me every minute." He slid into her and groaned. "So soft and sweet. I could cum on the spot, Lila."

Lila quivered around him and he pushed deeper inside. She thought she would die when he pulled out and rammed himself back inside her. He repeated the process over and over, driving her way past her breaking point. Her fingernails scraped against his back and she bit his shoulder. Her legs wrapped around him and locked him into place. "So help me, Karter Knight, if you don't stop teasing me I'm going to scream."

He chuckled. "But I like making you scream, Lila."

A rage filled her, one she did not understand. She pushed him off her and tackled him to the bed. The raw longing inside her was making her mad for him. Lila wasn't entirely sure of the mechanics at the moment. She looked into his eyes and begged him. "Help me, Karter."

He shuddered under her as his hands grabbed onto her ass. He parted her legs and guided her down onto his cock. As she sunk onto him he groaned loudly. "That's it, Lila. Slowly."

"Not likely." She moved herself up and down the length of him, taking her pleasure without a thought for his own. When his hands came up to cup her breasts, she whimpered.

"That's right, Lila. Take it. God, yes."

He tweaked her nipple and she came undone on top of him as the lights exploded behind her eyes. She was ready to topple over on top of him, but Karter held her up. He rode her orgasm hard and fast, his ass bouncing on the bed below her. When he came inside her he shouted her name.

"Lila!"

She could have sworn she heard a howl in that one word, but she must have imagined it. When he gathered her against

121

him, she snuggled on top of him. Her insides were still pounding dangerously as her body craved so much more.

"Are you pouting?" Karter chuckled.

"No," she lied.

"Yes, you are. What's the matter, Lila?"

She sighed. "I just...I'm still...."

"Ready to go?" he answered for her.

"I'm throbbing in places I didn't know had a pulse."

He stiffened beneath her. "Lila...."

"Did I say something wrong?" She sighed in disappointment. "I have a lot to learn. Like...." She licked his skin and nibbled slightly. "Exactly how long do I have to wait before—"

"You're insatiable," Karter teased her.

"It's not my fault that you're irresistible." She nibbled on his nipple and he growled.

"Lila...." His words were a warning.

"Yes, Karter?"

"You're playing with fire, love." His eyes met hers and she saw the gold sparks behind them.

"I'm not afraid of your wolf. Can he feel this?" Lila wrapped her hand around his cock and stroked it slowly.

"Yes...." His breath came in short gasps.

"Will he ever...?" How did Lila ask her next question without sounding completely stupid?

"He can only experience sex in the human form, Lila. So when we do this, he gets all the satisfaction he needs."

"So I get to have two at once?" She nibbled on her bottom lip and fluttered her eyelashes at him.

"Yes." He grinned at her.

"And Keelan...does he ever take over?" She whispered.

Karter's eyes showed his shock. "How do you know his name?"

"Am I not supposed to? I just...." Lila didn't how she knew it. It seemed to be second nature to her.

"No. I mean yes, you can know it. I just don't go around speaking it." He flinched as her hand squeezed him hard. "And he does like to take over, although I'm always present."

"I don't suppose he'd like to...."

Karter's eyes flashed and a loud roar erupted from his lips as he rolled her off him. Lila's breath caught in her throat when he ran his nails over her nipples. The beast inside was ready and willing. He tried to reason with his beast, but Karter was losing the battle. His hands gripped her bottom and pulled her off the bed as he pushed deep inside her.

Her breath caught in her throat as he took her fast and hard. She felt the waves start to rise as she came hard against him. This drove him even wilder as his cock continued to push her past the breaking point. This was no slow ride, as he took her over and over. When he finally came hard against her, Lila had lost all will to think. As he withdrew slightly, she winced. She had loved every minute, but was starting to feel the after affects from their lovemaking.

"You're hurt." His blue eyes were filled with regret. "I shouldn't have—"

Lila pulled his face down for a kiss. "I'm just sore, Karter. I imagine that is normal when you have this much sex so fast. I'm fine."

He sighed against her. "You're sure?"

She ran her fingers through his hair. "Very."

"You must be hungry." He nuzzled her nose with his own. "Let me make some food for us."

"You need to go shopping," she reminded him.

"Then let me bring something back for you." He grinned at her.

"Fine. I need to take a shower anyway." When she saw his thoughtful smile, she pushed him with her hands. "Go get food. You can always explore those thoughts later, Karter."

"Promise?" His blue eyes twinkled.

She pulled his mouth down to hers and sighed against him as his tongue slid into her mouth. Running a finger down his spine, she pictured his body covered in hot water. As much as that thought sent her imagination racing, she knew that her body needed to heal slightly. "Much later?"

"Poor baby."

"Poor *hungry* baby. Go get me food!"

"Yes, ma'am." He slid off her and went to retrieve his clothes.

He left her there to linger in her aftermath, feeling content for the first time in her life. Lila was not regretting her choices, not one bit. Her body was finally settling down as she relived some of the last moments in her head. As much as she loved how he made her feel, her thoughts turned to the problem at hand. She was going to have to find a way to put an end to the entity that was haunting Witch's Hollow, especially if it meant she could keep Karter alive.

Chapter 15

Lila took a shower and got ready for the day. She had a lot to do. A new book to edit, as well as trying to find a way to meet with Virginia Vinson. If she could talk Karter into it, she wanted to check on Taela too. Lila felt an unusual connection with the child. She was actually kind of sad that she hadn't had the chance to say goodbye.

First things first, she took her laptop out and sat down on the couch. Pulling up the latest book, she spent the next half hour working through her edits, wondering just how long Karter was going to be gone. Her stomach was really starting to grumble at her.

As if on cue, a car pulled into the drive. She set her computer down on the table and went to go greet him, but was surprised to find a woman who looked like she was in her early twenties, a blonde with legs that did not seem to stop. She was quite possibly the most beautiful woman that Lila had ever seen. When she rang the doorbell, Lila was trapped in between trying to figure out if she should answer the door or if she should pretend she wasn't home.

The choice was taken from her, because at that moment, Karter pulled up in the drive. Lila went to the living room and peered out from the side, hoping neither one of them could see her. Karter got out of the car and walked over to the woman. Lila couldn't be sure what his intent was, but she could see that the woman was clearly there for a reason. She felt bad for watching, but she couldn't seem to look away.

"Julia, what are you doing here?" Karter ran a hand through his hair as if her presence had clearly affected him.

The woman, Julia, slid closer to him and wrapped her arms around his neck. Before Lila knew it, she was watching her mate kissing another woman. When he stepped back slightly, Julia reached out and grabbed his crotch. Karter stopped moving.

Lila gasped when the woman slid up against him again. This time her tongue slid into his ear, and Karter didn't seem to be pushing her away. Lila felt her heart leap out of her chest and crash onto the floor, as if he had ripped it out himself. Everything up until this point had been exactly as she ever dreamt it would be. She felt like everything he had told her was a lie. How could she not have seen this coming?

This was the reality she should be used to, the one where a beautiful woman would turn his head much easier than hers would. Karter had told her that no other woman had come here before. Obviously, that had been a lie. She watched him lead her around the back of the house, not caring to watch any further. To do this with her in the house, it just...she could not understand why he would do that.

Lila was glad she hadn't unpacked her bag. She raced

upstairs and pulled it off the dresser it was sitting on. Lila peered out the back window and saw the two were still fairly distracted. Karter was attempting to push her hands away, but Lila wasn't falling for it. She knew he had far more experience than most men, never really attaching himself to anyone. Maybe this was the one who had gotten away. She was clearly a much better match for him.

A tear fell down her face as she touched the bite on her throat. Happily ever after was just an illusion after all. She had fallen for it, too. A bitterness rose up inside her. Why had he even wasted his time on her?

Lugging the suitcase down the stairs, she winced when it banged loudly at the bottom. Lila didn't want him to hear her go. There was nothing he could say to her that would keep her there.

As she slung the laptop bag over her shoulder, she felt a burning sensation. Lifting her hand up to her throat, she winced when she felt the scratches that had showed up after her dream. She remembered the lifeless body on the floor and shuddered. That thing was coming for her, she knew it. No matter how hurt or angry she felt, if Karter was not with her, she would be able to keep him alive.

She put her hand on the window and sighed. The woman was now sitting on his lap, as if it was second nature for her. Lila saw Karter turn to look at her, but she turned away before he could see her pain.

Tears fell down her face. This was the way it was always going to end; maybe that was why she couldn't see the dream any further before. Some things were not meant to be, no matter how much she wanted them. She put her things in the back seat of her car as quietly as possible. Whether he heard her leave or not, Lila didn't care. She drove as fast as she could down the drive, not bothering to look back.

Lila wasn't even sure where she was driving to, as the road winded left here and there. She made a left turn and followed the next road to the end. When she found herself pulling into a house she did not recognize at all, Lila did not understand why she was drawn to it.

She turned her car off and opened her door. Walking up to the front door, she barely got the chance to knock when Brina Knight pulled it open. "Good morning, Lila."

"Brina?" she whispered in surprise. "I'm not even sure how I got here."

"You look upset. Is everything all right?" Brina looked at her speculatively.

Lila really didn't know the woman standing before her, but she needed a friend, anyone who might understand. "I...I just...."

"What did he do?" Killian was right behind her.

"I...I think this was a mistake. I'm not even sure how I got here." She saw that the two-story house looked similar to Karter's, except for the garage was attached. Did they all have houses like this? She shook her head and turned away. "I'm sorry. This was a mistake. I'm going to go."

Killian picked up the phone that was ringing in his pocket. He looked over at Lila. "It's my jackass brother."

"Don't you dare tell him she's here, Killian."

Killian snorted. "Bri, you know good and well he already knows."

"You tell him I'm going to castrate him if he even thinks

about walking in this house." Brina reached for Lila's hand. "Inside, now. I'm sure he'll be here in five minutes. Better retreat while you can."

"I doubt it. He looked pretty occupied when I left."

Lila followed Brina into the house. She reached for the bite that should have made her feel complete and closed her eyes.

"Oh, my word. What did he do to you?" Brina saw the other red marks on her throat.

"No, he didn't do that." She held her hand up defensively.

"Well, he sure did that though." Brina pointed to the teeth marks.

Lila's choked up slightly. "Can we reverse it?"

Brina sighed. "Sit, Lila. Tell me what my fool brother-in-law did."

Lila heard some shouting outside and shrank into a couch. The tears fell down her face as she put her head in her lap. "I fell for it. All of it."

"What?"

"The whole one mate for the rest of his life. He made me feel like the only woman in the world. I've never felt...no man ever." Her fingers made tight fists as she thought about all the things that had happened the night before. Memories she would have been happy to carry with her the rest of her life had he not flaunted that woman in front of her like that.

"Right. And then what happened?" Brina was pursing her lips thoughtfully.

"Some blonde with legs up to her neck showed up this morning." Lila crossed her arms over her chest. "She was all over him. And he didn't seem to push her away. Why would he want me if he could have her? I think her name was —"

"Julia?" Brina looked around for little ears. "That bitch again? Damn it, Karter."

Lila heard the door rattle as Karter tried to get past Killian. She closed her eyes and tears fell down her face. Pain and fear were taking their turns cycling across her mind. "Maybe he should have chosen her."

Brina got up from the armchair and went to the door. Lila heard her voice over the noise outside. "You jackass. You're scaring her."

"I need to talk to her, Brina." His voice sounded frenzied.

"What you need to do is take yourself off my porch, Karter Knight, or I'm picking up the phone and calling your mother."

"You wouldn't."

"Try me." Brina's voice was shaking.

"I don't understand why she left. Everything was fine." Karter sounded genuinely confused.

"Killian, a little help please." She gestured for him to come closer and she whispered something in his ear.

"Seriously? Fuck. Let's go, Karter. She's going to need some time." Killian grabbed him by the collar and shoved him forward. "You're such an asshole sometimes."

"What did I do?" he asked in confusion.

Lila sighed in relief when she heard Karter's car leave the drive. When Brina returned to the room, she shook her head. "There are things you need to know, Lila."

"I have to go. I can't stay here." Lila had come here to find a way to break the curse over the Vinson house. That was what she would put her time and effort into. Then she planned to leave and never come back.

"Wherever you go, he will follow you, Lila. You're mated for life," Brina tried to caution her.

"Really? I'm not the one who has the problem with that. He's the one who — "

"Mama?" A small voice called through the door.

"Come on in, lovely. Lila's here."

The toddler came running through the door and launched herself into Lila's lap unexpectedly. "Auntie!"

Lila's breath caught in her throat. God, how she wished that could be true, but now her whole world was off kilter. A tear caught in her eye and she tried to hold it back. "Good morning, Sophie."

"Where's Karkar?" She asked her.

Lila's lips wobbled slightly. "Work?"

"Oh." Her lips opened in a large o-shape.

"How would you like to go see Nana?" Brina suggested.

"Nana!" Sophie hopped off her lap and started to dance around the room as she chanted "Na-na, Na-na."

"Let's go get you dressed."

Lila watched the pair of them and put a hand to her own belly. What it would be like to have a child just as beautiful. She had never known how much she wanted that before. A little child with blonde hair and crystal blue eyes. Lila was fairly certain that would never happen now. If any part of her tried to tell her it was for the best, she was going to lose her mind. How cruel for fate to dangle the only thing she'd ever wanted in front of her, only to have it yanked right out of her reach.

"I'm just going to take her to the inn. Please stay. I promise

Killian will keep him away. When I get back, I'll tell you all about Julia."

Lila nodded at her with a half-smile. She wasn't sure that she wanted to hear about the woman who had practically climbed into his lap right on the spot. And yet, there was a part of her that wanted to fight just a little. He had come right after her. Did that mean something?

Chapter 16

When Brina left, Lila was trying to keep herself from leaving. Every inch of her wanted to run as fast as she could and as far away as possible. She stood up and paced the room. What was she going to do? What could she do? The air was starting to feel stagnant inside the house.

Lila went to the back door and let herself out. Her feet walked with no destination in mind, just one right after the other. Before she knew it she was surrounded by earth and sky. Lila sat down on the grass and pulled her knees up to her chest. Taking her shoes and socks off, she let her feet touch the ground. The energy of the earth below seeped into her skin. Closing her eyes, she took in a deep calming breath.

Help us.

The whispers started for the first time that day. When she had been at Karter's the only one who had come in was Sera. No one else had bothered her, which had been nice for a change. Lila never had that much peace. Lila sighed, suddenly feeling very selfish. She had not come here for anything else but saving the spirits that had been trapped. Now, she was worried that the entity would bring destruction to those that she cared about. Lila had to do something, even if it meant putting everything she desired deep down inside her.

Standing up, Lila called out for Sera. "Where are you?"

Here.

Lila saw a white glow just a few feet ahead of her and took off in that direction. "Show me."

The white light led her deeper into the forest to a place where the trees started to rot before her. She tripped over a root and fell to her knees. Lila saw a drop of fresh blood and knew that something horrible had happened here.

Was this where Sera had been killed? She couldn't help but wonder what the authorities were doing to investigate. What could they do? From what she learned from Sera last night, her face was mutilated. It must have looked like she was mauled by some animal. Was it trying to mimic a wolf attack? That could be bad for the Knight pack if that were the case.

Lila felt drawn to the path that was barely visible. Just beyond the darkest tree, it led deeper into the forest to a place Lila knew was unsafe. Every inch of her told her to turn around, but Lila couldn't resist the pull forward. Like a magnet tethered to her belly button, it propelled her forward. Dead tree limbs littered the ground. Lila looked up and saw a few stick figures hanging down from the limbs. A few of them were painted with dried blood. Lila fought the urge to rip them down from the trees. Reaching up, she felt a darkness that almost eroded the light from her fingertips.

Lila shivered. Had that thing been made here? Was it

called forward from one of the vortexes near Witch's Hollow? Had the magical ley lines created this problem? Was it manmade? So many questions filtered through her head at once. None she would have the answer to.

She forced herself to move forward, closing her eyes as the void circled around her. Lila was being led somewhere else. This place was only part of the whole. The leaves crackled under her feet, like dead carcasses cast down below her. A wicked laugh echoed inside her head. It was amused at her fear, a fear that was almost crippling her the more she walked into the woods.

Lila stopped in front of a large boulder. Reaching down, she wiped the dirt away. There was something etched in the stone. "What is this?"

She touched the symbols on the stone and closed her eyes. She saw a flash of something in her mind. A doll. It laughed at her as its head revolved around on its neck. The eyes opened and closed, revealing the dark black marbles that had been placed in its sockets. Was that the doll that had been passed down in the Vinson family?

She heard the swish of something behind her, and her eyes shot open. Lila turned to face whatever was in front of her. A dark shadow-like creature was standing before her, if those were actual legs. Lila wasn't even sure that it was a physical being—it seemed trapped between life and death. She heard Sera's screams when it opened its mouth. Lila knew that Sera was no longer able to reach the light. Her soul was trapped in an infinite loop by the thing that was trying to grow into a much stronger power. This thing that collected spirits, was it here or there? Lila had no idea where the fight was supposed to begin, only that she needed more time to put all the pieces together.

"I'm not afraid of you," she shouted at it, praying that it didn't sense the fear in her heart.

You should be.

Lila threw up a shield around her as the creature threw itself at her. She fell as the force pushed her backwards. Her neck started to burn as the demon broke through her shield. Invisible hands wrapped around her throat, and Lila screamed as loud as she could, knowing no one would hear her. She was out here by herself, a mistake that would cost her life.

A snarl erupted behind her and the black mass backed away slightly, the grip on her throat lessening, but Lila could not get any air into her lungs. She heard a growl and gnash of teeth as the wolf sprang forward. Her eyes fluttered as she collapsed on the ground, her breath coming in loud gasps as she reached for her throat. When strong arms wrapped around her, Lila tried to fight them off. She didn't want him here.

"Damn it, Lila. Let me help you."

She couldn't speak, even though she wanted to scream at him. Her hands tried to push him away, but he was far too strong for her weakened state. Lila relaxed in his arms and looked up at him. His eyes were troubled, but she wasn't falling for it. She glared at him and tried to talk, but ended up coughing.

"Save your strength."

If he told her she was going to need it, Lila would scratch his eyes out. She found her strength and shoved him away from her as hard as she could. Realizing that her shirt had gotten ripped in the fight, she crossed her arms over her chest and looked away from him. She willed herself to feel nothing when she looked up at him.

"I'm not going to ravage you."

She held her chin up in anger. Damn right he wasn't going to ravage her. Lila pushed up from the ground and stood up defiantly. She knew he wanted to carry her, but she didn't want him to touch her at all. Lila tried to take a step and fell over as a sharp pain toppled her. Her ankle was throbbing painfully.

She winced as Karter's hands touched it, partly because it hurt like hell and partly because his hands had sent a shiver of desire racing through her. Lila looked away from him, willing her pride to keep her safe from his charm.

"Is she okay?" Killian called from the tree line.

"Her ankle is hurt. I don't think it's broken." Karter reached down to lift her up and she slapped his hands away. "Lila, you can't walk on this."

She crossed her arms over her chest and clamped her mouth shut. Her anger was well past the breaking point. Lila pushed up from the ground again, and this time put very little weight on the tip of her foot. She hopped as far as she could before she admitted defeat.

When Karter scooped her into his arms, she saw the amusement in his eyes. Lila reach through his shirt and latched onto his nipples, twisting them as hard as she could. He almost dropped her. "Okay. It's not funny."

Killian chortled with glee. "It is now!"

Lila glared at him and pointed at him threateningly. A slight electric spark shot from her fingertip. She was so angry she was near spitting. Coughing loudly, she forced the words out. "I hate you."

Karter's body flinched beneath her and she saw the pain in his eyes. Lila should have felt better about it, but she instantly regretted her words. Tears fell from her eyes as he carried her through the woods. Her teeth were almost destroying her lips, she had worried them so much.

When they reached the house, Brina came flying outside as fast as her feet could carry her. "You had us so worried."

Karter sat her down on the bench outside and tried to touch her face. She looked away from him, not trusting herself to look into his eyes. "Lila, please."

"Go away," she coughed as her throat threatened to collapse on her.

"Karter...." Brina put a hand on his arm. "Go. I'll take care of her."

"But—"

"So help me, Karter Knight, if you don't go right now, I will toss your ass out myself." Brina rose to her full height and he backed away.

"I'm not staying away, Lila. We will talk." His eyes flashed golden, as if Keelan were wanting to have his say too.

"Bully," she grumbled as he walked away.

I love you, Lila. His words whispered across her mind.

Liar, she answered. Lila saw him falter in his steps slightly, but he continued to walk away from her. When he was no longer in sight, Lila looked up at Brina helplessly. Tears fell down her face and choking sobs were barely audible. She gasped for air and Brina pulled her into her arms.

"Girl, I feel you. They're a handful and a half. Karter's

like three handfuls. You've got your work cut out for you." Brina's hug was filled with glowing light. "Let me get you some water."

Lila waited outside in the sunlight, and while it was warm outside, she was surrounded by an icy cold she could not fight off. She couldn't stop the tears from flowing, and the relief came from an unexpected place.

Killian put his hand in hers. "He's not always an asshole."

Lila doubted that. She narrowed her eyes on him and saw the rueful smile he gave her.

"Okay, maybe he is more often than not, but he's been changing this past year."

Lila looked away from him. She gestured to her legs all the way up to her chin and twirled her hair in her fingers. Her lips mouthed one name. *Julia.*

"Yes, Julia. It doesn't make any sense to me, Lila." He gestured to her throat. "He clearly chose you, but something always seems to happen whenever she comes around."

She rolled her eyes. Lila knew exactly what happened whenever she came around. He dropped everything and went running to her like she was a dog in heat. She hated to think about what she would have seen if she had stayed at his house any longer this morning.

"Lila, listen to me. He didn't even know she came this morning."

She narrowed her eyes on him. What was he saying? Lila tried to form words, but she could only get one out. "What?"

"I know my brother. I know his wolf, sometimes better than he does. I'm the alpha. It's my job. They were both confused."

"That's no surprise. That woman has been stringing him along for years now." Brina clucked her tongue.

"Whenever she shows her face, it's almost like he's under a spell or something." Killian shook his head ruefully.

"She can't be that good." Brina rolled her eyes.

Lila looked down at the ground. Maybe she was that good. She'd certainly had more experience than Lila. Why would he want her, if he could have that?

"Oh dear, we're not helping. How would you like to get some rest, Lila?" suggested Brina.

Rest...not like it would work, but she would do anything if it meant she didn't have to stay here listening to them any longer. They helped her get inside to the spare bedroom and onto the bed. She heard them arguing in the other room. Killian thought Lila should be staying with Karter, trying to work it out, and Brina was adamant that Lila not leave.

Lila sighed as she closed her eyes. The day had certainly taken its toll on her. More tears flowed down her face and she cried until exhaustion finally crept over her, even though she was terrified of falling asleep.

Chapter 17

As she slept, Lila was tormented with rotating faces that she didn't recognize. Their voices called out to her, but she couldn't understand them. She was trapped within an abyss she could not seem to climb her way out of. Lila watched Karter die over and over in her mind, mourning his loss every time. The wave of sadness inside her took her will to live right from her body, but the frequency in which the images passed convinced her that this could not be real.

At one point the voices sounded familiar, and while she could hear them, Lila was unable to respond.

"What do you mean she won't wake up?" Karter's voice was almost livid. "I knew I shouldn't have left her."

"I've tried everything I know how to do." Brina's voice was filled with concern.

Lila wanted to tell them she was right there, that she could hear them, but she just could not seem to reach them. Was Karter crying?

"I'll let you have a moment." Brina cleared her throat and

Lila could feel her hand on hers briefly before she left.

Lila felt his lips on her forehead and something wet fell down onto her face. "Please be okay."

Lila heard the plea in his voice, and while she wanted to run toward it, her heart wasn't sure she could trust it. She felt him slide into the bed next to her, but her limbs would not move. Nothing seemed to work. Lila felt him wrap his arms around her, and the bed shook as he cried into her hair. Lila had never heard a man cry before, but she felt his sorrow wrap around her like a bitter fog. Whatever he had done to her, she couldn't stand to feel his grief.

"Don't run away, Lila. Run back to me," he begged her.

Light shone down on the world inside her like a beacon showing her the way. Lila was crawling through a crypt of bodies buried so deep within the ground it was hard to climb over them. Her foot slipped on a skull and she heard the unnerving crunch of bones beneath her. She shuddered and tried to keep moving forward. The stillness around her was deafening.

This must be where he trapped them. Lila refused to be his next victim, no matter how much control he thought he had over her. She was not going to be trapped inside like one of his victims. Lila had a life to live and people to protect.

"Come back...," Karter's voice whispered to her. She heard it echo around inside her. Lila tried to reach out for him, but all she could do was follow his light.

Karter. She called out to him, praying he could hear her. He did not reply. Lila saw his light fading and knew she had to push herself harder. She felt a bony hand reach out and grab her leg. Lila tried to shake it off, but more bones started to rise up from the pitch below.

"This is not happening!" she screamed. Her hands opened up and a crackling blue light sizzled between them. It was not going down like this. Not today. She blasted the hand that was latched on to her and watched it shatter before her. As the bones reanimated around her, Lila sent blast after blast at them before racing toward what was left of the light.

When she finally opened her eyes, it was pitch black outside. Lila moved her legs and found the throbbing reminder of the injury she'd received earlier. Someone had taken great care as they'd wrapped it up. Karter was no longer holding her—he was nowhere to be found. Even though she was so mad at him, a larger part of herself needed to know that he was okay.

Lila found her shoes near the bed and slid them over her feet. Her left ankle was wrapped, which made her shoe a little tighter, but she would manage. She was dressed in a long white shirt that smelled a lot like Karter. Had he helped dress her? And how long was she asleep? Lila still didn't know why she had not been able to wake up. That was a matter for another time.

The house was silent as Lila made her way slowly out the door. She didn't know where Karter was until she heard a lonely howl. His sorrow pulled her to him. Lila was careful not to bump into anything as she walked. When she made it to the outside of the house, she saw a large walking stick that had been intricately carved. Hoping they wouldn't mind, Lila used the stick to take some of the weight off her foot.

Making her way to the edge of the trees, Lila listened for another sign from him. She wanted to call out to him, but she was afraid he wouldn't hear her. Another howl erupted far inside the forest. Lila moved as fast as her injured feet could carry her. When she found a large boulder in the middle of a clearing, she inched over to it to take a break.

Looking up at the moon, she saw the large white orb in the sky. The light streamed down on her and she breathed it in. The full moon was powerful. It replenished the soul and brought a peace that had eluded her while she slept. As much as she wanted to fight the being that had targeted her, right now all she wanted was Karter.

Karter. She reached out to him, not knowing whether he could find her or not. Closing her eyes, she wrapped her arms around herself and shivered against the cold breeze. Looking up at the stars, she willed him to find her. Listening for his howl, she felt a tear fall down her face when she did not hear it again. He was gone.

"*Lila....*" His voice whispered across the clearing as if he could not believe she were there.

It was so faint, Lila didn't think she had heard it. It had to be just an illusion of the night. Lila put her head in her knees and more tears fell down her face. When his voice came again, it was right at her side.

"Don't cry. Please don't cry."

Lila turned to find him standing at her side. He did not make a move toward her, which made her wonder if he were even real. She reached out to his arm and pinched it hard. "You're real."

He grimaced slightly. "Yes. So are you."

"Karter...." She didn't know what to say to him. He stood just out of her reach, as if he were trying to decide whether he should reach out to her or not. Her anger had seemed so righteous before, but now it was lost on the wind. "I don't—"

"Hate me?" He asked her softly.

"No." She reached for his hand and waited to see if he would give it to her. When he didn't, she looked away from him. Maybe he was just an illusion after all.

Karter knelt on the ground before her and reached up to wipe the tears from her face. His eyes were a turbulent blue, the eyes of a man who had been mourning. "I thought I lost you."

"I'm still here," she smiled at him. For how long, she did not know. With that thing chasing after her, she was on borrowed time. Something had to give very soon.

"No thanks to me."

"What?" Lila blinked in confusion.

"You were running from me, Lila. It was my fault."

Was that what he thought? Lila climbed off the rock and put her arms around his neck. She sent every inch of her loving energy into his body, hoping he could understand what she could not put a voice to. "I wasn't running from you."

"Julia…." He looked tortured. "I didn't…."

Lila looked into his eyes and saw a lost soul, a man who wasn't sure if she would believe him. She put her nose against his and took a deep breath for courage. What he needed now was forgiveness. "Tell me about Julia."

"I don't know what to say, Lila. I can't even remember how we met. Every time she gets near me, it's like my mind isn't my own." He put a hand on her face.

"Maybe she was supposed to be your—"

"Don't say that." He pushed away from her. "That woman

is not my mate."

Lila felt her neck for his mark, but it had faded beneath the surface. Had he even marked her? Or had that just been a dream? "Have you slept with her, Karter?"

"Before you?" He did not turn to face her.

"Yes, Karter. Before, after…ever?" Lila didn't want the truth, not really, but she had to let him tell it.

"Yes."

She shivered slightly and tried to let go of the sadness his words brought. "Which?"

"Which?" He turned to her with a confused look on his face.

"Before or after?" Tears were threatening to take her over.

"Before. Never again." Karter looked as if he were practicing self-restraint.

"Good." Lila felt anger growing inside her at the thought of that woman putting her hands on her man, and she clenched her fists.

"You're angry."

"*Yes,*" she whispered as her body started to shake. Lila was not used to these emotions, and had nowhere to put them.

"Hit me," he told her.

"What?" His words broke through her burning haze.

"Hit me, Lila. I can take it." Even so, his voice was tortured.

"No." She held her chin up.

"Why not?" He asked her quietly.

"I could never hurt you." Not on purpose. And she realized in that moment that neither could he. There was something going on that was out of his control, something that Lila would have to get to the bottom of. Lila put her hands on his face and sighed. "We're quite the pair, aren't we?"

"What do you mean?" His eyebrows rose curiously.

"Broken."

Her word caught him off guard, and Lila understood why. His family saw him differently than he was. They saw the prankster, the playboy who was always at the center of whatever joke was happening at the time. His ploys were for attention and to hide the bitter truth he held deep inside. The smile he kept on his face was to hide the emptiness he felt. It masked the self-conscious part of himself, the part that thought he was unlovable. How did she know? Because they were kindred spirits.

"I see you, Karter. You don't have to pretend with me."

His fingers rubbed against her cheek. "I see you too, Lila. You are the most beautiful thing I've ever seen."

Lila looked into his eyes, and all she could see was the truth. This man loved her. That was something worth fighting for. Heaven help the woman who ever thought to get between them. He belonged to her, and she was going to make damned sure that woman knew it if she ever brought her skanky ass around him again. Lila may seem meek and passive, but heaven help the person who tried to hurt anyone she loved. Loved. She loved him, and that knowledge was the greatest gift she could have.

Lila pulled his mouth down to hers and sighed against his mouth when his lips covered hers. One soft gentle kiss and her world came alive before her eyes. "Can we go home, Karter?"

"Anything." Karter scooped her up in his arms and started to carry her.

"I can walk, Karter." Lila shook her head ruefully. Did he expect to carry her all the way home? She knew he was strong, but there had to be some limits.

"Yes, but this way I can make sure you don't run." He nipped her ear playfully and she giggled.

"I couldn't even if I wanted to." She snuggled her head into his neck and sighed in contentment. Lila felt a peace emanating from him. She knew the feeling at once. He *was* home to her. There were quite a few things they were going to have to figure out.

Chapter 18

Lila was surprised at how close they were to his house. She wondered if all the Knight properties were that close to each other. Did they own all this land?

When they were closer to the house, Karter finally set her down. It was then that she realized that she had left the walking stick in the clearing.

"I left the walking stick behind, Karter." Lila felt a little guilty about leaving it there.

"Don't worry. Killian will get it," he assured her.

"Are you sure? It was beautiful."

"He's got ten more of them in his garage. That's what he does in his spare time. Or when Brina's about to rip him a new one, which is at least half of the time."

"So you're all a handful?"

He gave her a boyish grin. "My poor mother...."

"I can only imagine." Lila used his shoulder to hold part of her weight as she walked up the small path through the garden.

Karter opened the back door for her and helped her inside. "In you go."

"Thank you."

The minute she entered she realized the house was in disarray. It looked like Karter had torn the house apart in a frenzy.

"It was a rough few days here," he apologized.

"How long was I asleep?" Lila had no idea how long she had been asleep. One of the last things she remembered was being attacked in the forest by a shadow creature. Had she pushed him away then? It seemed so long ago.

"Four days." His face fell and he turned away from her. "It was bad, Lila."

She sat down on the couch and sighed. "Come, Karter. Tell me what happened."

"You stopped breathing three times, Lila. Almost like you wanted to...."

"Die?" Had she? She didn't think so, but he didn't have any idea the fight that was going on inside her at the time. Had her pain made her an easy target? Was her connection to him a strength or a weakness to be manipulated by whatever demon was haunting her?

"I hurt you."

"Yes. You did." Sugar coating it wasn't going to change how she had felt or what had happened. Her understanding of the situation had changed, though. While she hadn't sorted it completely out yet, she did know that Karter had not intended for Julia to manhandle him the way she had. She was on her list of things to get to the bottom of. First, the demon. Then the harlot.

"I'm sorry." He was, too. It was displayed on every inch of his features. Karter had lived through hell while she had been trapped in the nightmare that would not end.

"How did they revive me?" Lila was actually glad they had not taken her to a hospital. Medical science could not fight the venomous magic she was being attacked with. Lila wasn't sure what she was going to do to make the demon disappear from this world, or if it was even possible to banish him.

"Mom and Brina stayed by your side. They tried to pull you out of your sleep, but you refused to budge."

"You thought I was running from you?" Lila put her head on his shoulder and sighed. She couldn't quite figure out why she felt like running from him so much. Fear of rejection? Her inability to believe that a man like him could love a woman like her? Both thoughts were a weakness that had been molded inside her from a young age, both things she seemed to have no control over. Lila wanted to erase those thoughts from her mind, but that took time and patience.

"Weren't you?"

Lila sighed. There was a lot to explain, some things that would not make sense. At the time, Lila thought she was running away from him, but deep down she was leading herself back to him without thinking. Her mind had brought her to a friend she didn't even know she had. "I was mad. I just needed time to regroup, Karter. It probably won't be the last time."

"And the forest?"

"I came here to find the demon that's chasing me, Karter. I know you think I came here just for you, but my life does exist outside of you."

"I know," he sighed.

"Do you?" Lila asked him. "What do you know about me, Karter?"

"Yes, you are a medium. You came here because you are…what are you doing?"

Lila shook her head. "You don't know much about me, do you?"

"I know what I need to know," he assured her.

"And what is that?"

"You are my mate."

Lila looked up at his face and saw a goofy grin on his face. She punched him in the arm. "Karter!"

"Fine…so we skipped a few steps. Or I was so distracted by your beauty that I wasn't listening."

"I have a college degree, Karter. I'm a freelance editor for Green Haven Publishing. Yes, I am a medium, and a solitary witch. I'm the youngest in my family, with two older siblings. My family was very religious, to the point where accepting my paganistic roots was impossible. My grandmother, pretty eccentric herself, took me in when I graduated college. I never knew she was a witch too."

"She sounds lovely."

"She was. I lost her six months ago, which is why I said I wish I had a family like yours. Blood isn't always thicker than water, you know." Lila couldn't look at him right now.

"My family is yours." Karter kissed the top of her head. "My mother is smitten with you, by the way. Brina thinks you've lost your mind a little, though."

"Why?"

"She thinks you deserve better." He ran a hand through

his hair and sighed. "She's probably right."

"She doesn't know you the way I do, Karter. I love you the way you are."

"Say that again." His eyes flashed golden hues before the turbulent ocean returned.

"That she doesn't know you—"

"The part where you said you love me."

"I didn't say that," she teased him.

"Liar."

Lila smiled at him and touched his face with her hands. "I love you, Karter. From the dream you were, to the man you've become."

"I love you too, Lila. The thought that I could lose you—"

"I'm not going anywhere as long as I can help it. But that thing, he has other ideas. When I was asleep, he manipulated my dreams. I lost count of all the ways I watched you die." She shivered as she recalled the most gruesome tortures. "And then when that passed, I heard you calling for me. You saved my life, Karter. I felt you here. If you had not been here, I might have given up. I don't want to live in a world where you no longer exist."

"My sweet Lila." His voice was filled with emotion. "I've never felt this way in my life. I want to deserve your love."

"You do, Karter. You make me see myself in a whole different light. You make me feel beautiful for the first time in my life."

"How sad that it took all this time for you to figure that out." He picked up her hand and kissed it softly.

Lila had the distinct impression that this was not the charm he used on other women. She made him softer, brought out the kindness in his eyes. It had been growing inside him in ways she knew he did not understand. Lila knew that feeling. It was the same thing for her. But instead of soft, she was learning to be brave, to fight for the things that she wanted most in this life, and right now that meant asking the harder questions. "Where do we go from here, Karter?"

"What do you mean?"

"This has all happened so fast, Karter. We're bound together, but...."

"Ah...." Karter caught on, thankfully. "Marriage?"

"Do mates...? I mean, are they...?" Why was this hard to talk about? In a normal relationship, people dated, then decided if they were compatible enough for marriage. She had no idea if marriage ever entered the picture. Lila thought that Brina and Killian were married, but that was merely an assumption at this point.

"That depends."

Lila felt her insides churn slightly. What could it depend on? Whether he wanted to be legally bound to her outside of the magic that brought them together? She was almost afraid to know what the answer was. Did she want that commitment? It was more of a religious one than anything else, right? Of course, for legal reasons, some kind of marriage certificate probably would need to be filed, maybe?

"I've done this horribly, Lila." Karter sighed deeply. "Knights are a rare breed. Our passion takes over and we forget that those who aren't suffering our affliction view life differently. We skip steps, important ones."

"Oh?" she whispered.

"Yes." Karter moved away from her and slipped from

the room. When he returned he had a small box in his hand. He knelt before her and took her hand. "My heart is yours, always and forever. The only life I want to live is the one where you're by my side, Lila. Will you be my mate, my companion, my wife? My sunrise and sunset? Accept me for my faults, because I come with too many to list?"

"Yes, I will." Lila wasn't sure when the tears had started.

Karter opened the box to reveal a simple white gold band with a large amethyst tear drop in the middle. There were small diamonds inlayed in the band. He slid the ring over her finger and kissed her hand. "As much as I feared that I had lost you, I still believed you would come back to me."

Lila leaned down and kissed him. Karter scooped her off the couch and pulled her onto his knee. He broke the kiss and let his forehead touch hers. "As much as I want you, you need your rest. I also need to make sure my brother knows you're here. They're worried about you too."

Lila smiled. "I'm sorry to make them worry, but it's nice to have people who care."

"Never fear. There will be days you wished they didn't care so much," he teased her.

"Never." She wrapped her arms around his neck. "Would you mind carrying me to bed?"

"That I can do, but don't get any ideas about ravishing me when we get there." His eyes twinkled, but there was a seriousness there too. He was in protective mode. She recognized it.

"You're no fun," she grumbled.

"Oh, I'm all kinds of fun, but you're not riding this rollercoaster until you're cleared."

"Rollercoaster?" Lila giggled. He was a little like that. There were times he made her want to throw her hands up and scream, other times when she wanted to grab onto him and hold on tight. Then there were the times where he made her world go tilt-a-whirl as they went on the loop de loop together. She could use a little of that. Lila started to plot the many ways she could try to make him act a little less like a gentleman. Unfortunately, she was pretty sure he would not give in to her tonight.

"Well, if you'd prefer a stallion…." He winked at her.

"How about a cook? You do have more than peanut butter, right?"

"Barely. I might have some soup in the cabinet."

"If you don't mind…." Lila hated making him wait on her, but she was starting to feel hungry.

"You have but to ask, Lila."

"Well, in that case, I'd like—"

"For food. I'm not going to take advantage of you." He was biting back a chuckle.

"But what if I take advantage of you?"

Karter's laughter filled the stairway. "I've completely corrupted you."

Lila didn't mind one bit. While there were still a fair number of bumps to work through, she was still more content than she'd been in a very long time. She looked down at the ring on her finger, enjoying the happy sparkle that grew deep inside her when she glanced at it.

Chapter 19

The next morning, Lila awoke to an empty bed. The sheets were cold to touch, which told her that Karter had not been in bed all night. In fact, she was pretty sure she had fallen asleep a little after she'd filled her stomach with food. Even though he wasn't near her, she had felt safe in the house. The horrible dreams that had plagued her were gone—for one night, at least. She couldn't help the fear that raced through her brain. If she didn't find a way to banish this evil, it could one day take the only thing she cared about, the mate who had claimed her when she thought she was destined to be alone. She would not let that thing take him away from her.

Lila pushed herself out of the bed and hopped to the bathroom. When she almost tripped in the doorway, she put pressure on her foot and found her ankle was not as painful as it had been. It was still awkward and sore, but she could put more weight on it than she had been able to a few days ago. That didn't mean she was able to run a marathon, but she could get back to work.

After getting ready for the day, Lila made her way down the stairs, one step at a time, using the rails to help alleviate some of the strain. When she reached the bottom of the stairs, Lila saw Karter curled up on the couch and her heart felt light. His bare chest was exposed, as the small blanket was not enough to cover all of his body. Part of her wondered how naked he was under that blanket. Walking over to him carefully, Lila knelt before him. She let her hand roam across his face, memorizing every aching detail with her fingertips.

When her hands roamed down his chest, Lila sighed. His heat was intoxicating, and she had barely even touched him. Was this how she would feel for the rest of her life? An aching need to be near him? To have him bring her to life when the world was cold and bitter? As her fingers grazed his nipples, she felt his muscles bunching under her touch.

"Lila...," he growled in warning.

"What?" she whispered innocently.

"You're playing with fire."

"Oh? Do you think I'm afraid of getting burned?" She wanted him to set her on fire with his touch, to build a torrent of desire inside her. Lila ached for his touch. Leaning over, she ran kisses across his face, purposefully skipping his mouth. When she nibbled on his ear, she felt him tense. "Do I get to take advantage of you now?"

Karter groaned, and she saw him trying to control himself. "You're hurt, Lila."

She licked his ear and bit him again. "I hurt so bad...."

"Where?" His voice was filled with concern.

"Everywhere." She ran her fingernail against his erect nipple and he shook slightly.

"Lila, I'm trying very hard to be a gentleman." He was almost shaking as gold light tried to push through his blues.

"Well, then you can help me with something." She kissed his neck and bit down hard, marking him the way he had marked her.

Karter almost wrenched himself off the couch as a low growl erupted from his throat. He sat up and ran a hand through his hair. "With what, Lila?"

"Tell me what you like. Let me please you." Lila wanted to learn his body the way he had hers. She climbed into his lap and ran a hand across his face. She nibbled his shoulder softly. "Soft, or...."

"God, yes. Definitely hard." His voice was a clear indicator that he was enjoying the attention.

"Karter?"

"Yes, Lila?"

"Please don't get too excited. I've got a lot to learn." She licked her lips and he shivered. "You're not afraid, are you?"

"Terrified," he whispered.

She ran a hand along his chin and leaned over to kiss him. At first her lips were soft against his, but desire jolted through her and she could not control it. Her lips were hard against his, pushing into him with every ounce of her longing. When he tried to master the kiss, she moved away. "Ah-ah. This is my turn, Karter."

Lila wanted to learn everything she could. What made him wild for her? How long would she last before she let him have his wicked way with her? Lila decide to leave her clothes on for now. With a barrier between them, she would be able to draw out this experience. She only hoped he didn't rip her clothes off her. Lila actually liked this outfit.

"What do you want me to do, Lila?" he asked her with a handsome grin. He was clearly on board with this now.

"Just tell me what you like." Lila kissed him again and let his tongue slide into her mouth. When she bit it, he groaned and gripped the couch beneath him. Lila sucked him hard into her mouth. Lila broke the kiss and looked into his eyes. "Do you like when I bite you? Or was it the sucking?"

Karter sucked in his breath at her words. "Both."

"Does that work everywhere?" She asked him curiously. Her fingers moved down his chest.

"Yes." He watched her eyes look further down. "Just what are you planning on doing, Lila?"

"I haven't decided yet." She nibbled on her bottom lip. "I mean, if you would rather I didn't—"

"Don't you dare stop, Lila." His voice was strained.

"All right, but it might take me awhile, Karter. There's a lot of ground to cover." Her mouth came down to his ear and licked it again. "Do you need a safe word?"

"Excuse me?" His voice was a little higher pitched now.

Lila ran her nail against his nipple and bit his ear. Her mouth moved down his neck and she moved the blanket away from his body. She gasped in surprise. "You're so hard." His erection jumped at the compliment and he grinned at her. Lila slid down his body and rubbed the tip of his cock with her fingers. "And soft."

"Lila...." His body jerked beneath her touch.

"Does that hurt?" she asked him curiously.

"No." He was speaking through gritted teeth.

Lila caressed his penis from the tip to the base, taking

in the veins that were popping up slightly. She gazed up at him and saw he was trying to keep himself in check. He was failing miserably. "That looks painful. Shall I kiss it and make it better?"

"I'm not sure you...oh my god, Lila." He almost fell off the couch when she ran small kisses up and down the length of his erection. "You're not going to—" He groaned as she took his cock into her mouth. "Apparently, yep...you're going to go there. Be careful not to—" Lila licked along the length of his scrotum and his breath caught in his throat. "Dear Lord, you're going to end this before it begins if you keep...."

Lila sucked one of the round balls into her mouth and reveled in the trembling waves that passed through his body. She had no idea that the scrotum could bring a man such pleasure. The more she drove him wild, the hotter she became. Lila loved the control she had over him.

"Gahhhh, Lila...."

She heard something rip and realized his nails had sliced through the couch cushions under him. Lila let go of him and pouted up at him. "Should I stop? You look like you're in pain."

Karter took in a deep breath, as if trying to control the beast inside him. "I'm fine, Lila."

"So I can keep going?" she asked hopefully.

His eyes softened and he took another breath. "I might need that safe word after all."

She licked her lips and smiled at him. "Can I?"

"Can you what?" Karter looked apprehensive.

"I mean, how do I...?" She sighed and bit her lip. "I think I'll just work it out."

"Work what out...." His last word was drawn out as Lila took his cock deep into her mouth. She ran her tongue along the length of it and massaged it. When she removed her mouth, she looked up at him. "Am I doing it right?"

"Are you plotting my death? I think you might just kill me." Karter ran a finger across her lips and closed his eyes.

"What should I do?" She tilted her head and waited for him to answer. "I want to please you, Karter."

"You do, Lila."

"You have to tell me what you like, Karter. Teach me." She was desperate for some guidance.

Karter sighed. "Take me into your mouth, Lila."

She did as he asked and sighed when he pumped into her mouth. As he did, she felt a hot desire pierce her. Nature took over as she sucked him hard, wanting to bring him to the brink. She ran her tongue up and down his cock as she took him with her lips. Lila released him and licked her lips. "Was that all right?"

"All right?" Karter was fighting a violent longing.

She pouted. "I guess I should practice some more."

"Oh, hell no." Karter put his hand over his crotch. "Not unless you want this to be over right now."

"Would it please you?" she asked him.

"Yes. No. Hell, I don't know. You're making it hard to think."

"Good. Maybe you think too much." Lila lifted her shirt over her head and tossed it on the floor. When Karter saw she wasn't wearing a bra underneath, his eyes flashed. "So, you like my breasts?"

He pointed to himself. "Man. Simple creature."

Lila stood up and slid her yoga pants down her hips, taking her panties with them. She looked down at her breasts. "So what do you like about them?" Lila ran her hand along the curve of her breast. "Is it the outside?" She didn't wait for him to answer. Running a finger around the outside of her areola, she watched his golden eyes transforming. "So you like here?"

Lila felt her areola hardening under her soft touches. She flicked her nipple with her finger and heard him suck in his breath. Taking both nipples in her hands, she squeezed them while he watched her. She saw him gripping the couch cushions painfully. If the cushions had been a living creature he would have squeezed the life out of them.

"What do you want, Karter?" She wanted him to feel the way he made her feel when he made her wild with desire for him.

"Come here, Lila." He reached out and pulled her into his lap. Looking down at her ankle, his features softened. "Is your ankle all right?"

"That not the part of me throbbing right now, Karter."

"I have definitely created a monster," he sighed before his mouth came down on hers.

His hands squeezed her ass as she moved her hips so that she rocked into his belly. She could feel his cock near her clit and she whimpered slightly. Rubbing herself against him, she felt a heat course through her body. Her nipples rubbed against his chest as he crushed her closer to him. Sensing her need, he pumped against her.

"Someone is awfully wet," he murmured against her lips.

"You make me leak," she giggled, but when he slid his

cock inside her, her breath caught in her throat. Lila was about to ask him another question.

"Yes, Lila. I like when you're on top, on bottom, sideways, upside down, and any way I can have you."

"Upside down?" Lila nibbled on her lip thoughtfully. "How does that...?"

His mouth captured hers, breaking her sentence off before she could say another word. His hands gripped her ass and he brought her up and down the length of him. She felt the pace he was setting and started to rock against him, taking him so deep inside her that she thought he would impale her. She arched her back and whimpered when he took her nipple into his mouth. His hands continued to guide her onto his cock, the silky sweet movement driving her well past her limits.

When she shuddered around him, he stilled his movements. Lila tried to stop her movements, to savor the moment, but he forced her to continue to push past her limits. The more she rode him the deeper the desire coiled inside her. A frenzy started to build, and all she could think about was taking him over and over inside her.

His grip over her bottom released as Lila started to ride him hard and fast. Her breath came in loud pants as she squeezed him hard inside her. He stopped pushing into her and let her take him however she wanted. Like her own personal joystick, he held himself in place. She saw his face strain as he fought the urge to take what he wanted from her. Lila hated that he was holding part of himself back, but she couldn't stop herself from going for more.

His hands squeezed her breasts hard as he held in his breath. "Take it, Lila. God, yes."

When she came hard against him, she felt something wet squirt between them. That was when Karter lost his control. He pumped deep and hard into her, ignoring the iron will he had tried to compose. He brought one of his hands between them and started to stroke her clit.

A jolt of electricity shot through her body as the slightest touch sent her over the edge. An excruciating fire blazed inside her as her finish was laced with pleasure and pain. The ache inside her was soothed the moment he came inside her.

Lila fell over on top of him and sighed against him. "I'm sorry."

"For what?"

"I didn't last very long," she pouted at him.

His chest shook with laughter. "You didn't last long? I'm the weak one."

Lila rubbed her nose against his neck. "Nothing about you is weak. I'm just pretty persuasive."

"You can persuade me any time you like, Lila."

She sighed against him. "I'm going to hold you to that, Karter."

Karter wrapped his arms around her and kissed the top of her head. "I love you, Lila."

"You better. You're stuck with me." Lila let her insides squeeze him and felt him jerk inside her. "So when is round two?"

"You're insatiable."

"I blame you," she teased him.

"I wish I could stay, Lila, but I have to get some work done today." His voice was filled with regret.

"Me too. Do you think you might be able to...?"

"Your car and your things are already outside, Lila. Promise me one thing?"

"What?"

"Stay out of the woods today?" His eyes were filled with concern for her safety.

"Fine."

She didn't want to go to the woods anyway. She needed to talk to Virginia Vinson to find out more about this doll that seemed tied to the darkness that haunted her. Climbing off his lap, Lila gathered her clothes. As she walked up the stairs, she felt his eyes on her and smiled. Walking around naked wasn't something she normally did, but when he was watching her like that, she thought maybe it was something she should do more often.

Chapter 20

Lila knew it might be smarter to stay put, but she was on a mission. She wanted to find out more about Virginia Vinson. She wasn't sure how everything was connected. Was that thing in the Vinson house the same thing that haunted these lands? And if so, how could it be in two places at once?

As she pulled into Rainer Homestead, Lila felt a shiver run up her spine. The scratches that had started to heal around her throat started to burn. It was not happy that she had come here. Lila walked over to the front desk and smiled at the woman behind it. "Good morning, I'm here to see Virginia Vinson."

"Yes, she was expecting you. Room 312."

She was? Lila was a little surprised by that admission. She refused to outwardly acknowledge it though. "Thank you."

Lila made her way down the hall once the woman buzzed her through. As she walked through the halls, she heard a handful of spirits reaching out to her, but she refused to acknowledge them. That was not what she had come here for today. Ignoring the slight pain as she walked on her foot, she made her way to room 312 and knocked on the door.

"Come inside, child."

Lila opened the door and saw the older woman sitting in an armchair next to the window. She was frail and thin, with wispy white hair that seemed to get away from the bun at the top of her head. "Are you Virginia?"

"Ginny, dearie. You must be Lila." She waved her over to her.

"How did you know that?" Lila wondered aloud.

"Oh dear, it's the witch in me, I suppose." Her cheeks had a rosy pink glow to them.

"Oh. I didn't know." Lila moved closer to her. "I had a few questions—"

"You want to know about the hauntings."

"Yes. What can you tell me about him?"

"Ezra?" Ginny asked her.

"Is that his name?" Lila shivered.

"Yes. Nasty little demon. I was lucky to escape him. I see you're not so lucky." The woman nodded to the scratches around her throat

"No. I had no idea what I was walking into."

"Most don't, but you're resilient. Others would have toppled before now."

"I've had my moments." Lila thought back to the battle inside herself. She had been lucky to claw her way out.

"You're a fighter. Which is good. He's not expecting the fight."

"Do you know...?"

"How to defeat him?" Ginny smiled knowingly. "That's

something I was never able to do. I'm afraid he will come for you soon enough."

Lila put a hand to her throat. "Not if I can help it."

"You must destroy the doll, Lila. It's the one thing that ties him to this world."

"How is he attacking both places?"

"His ties to the house are the same as the doll. I'm afraid I wasn't able to destroy it when I was younger. My powers were limited and I was afraid of the fight." Ginny sighed as she let her mind wander. "I just wanted to keep my children safe. I never thought about the rest of the world. I wasn't as altruistic as you. I wasn't able to save my granddaughter. Now I'm afraid my great granddaughter is in danger. I believe you've met her."

The only child she had met was the one that Karter had brought home with him. "Taela?"

"Yes. All these years I've spent trying to protect my own, and he still managed to take them down. One by one, while I watched from this prison my body has kept me in."

"Is he after Taela?"

"No, but that sadistic woman, her grandmother, is. I'm afraid Gertrude's going to hurt her. I know Sera would want her to be with someone who understands her."

"She's a beautiful child. Extremely talented."

"Will you take her?" Ginny asked her.

"I'm sorry?" Lila was confused as to what Ginny was asking her.

"She needs a proper mother, Lila. One who will teach her the ways. She needs a witch like you, not that old orangutan she's been left with. Speaking of which, here they come."

When Taela charged into the room, the little girl had tears sparkling in her eyes. She saw Lila inside the room and launched herself at her. Lila had the distinct impression she was holding on for dear life. "Lila!"

"Taela!" scolded the older woman. "I'm sorry. We're working on her manners." The woman yanked the little girl away from Lila and glared at Taela. Lila saw the child shrink under the woman's weight. "Sit down."

"Yes, Grandmother."

"Heaven help me. That child is a handful. I'm not sure what I'm going to do with her. I'm not in the best of health, but no one else will take her."

"Oh, do shut up, Gertrude." Ginny's fingers clenched the armchair and Lila saw a sharp spark in her eyes that reminded her a lot of Karter. Was she a werewolf too?

"She's a piece of work, Virginia. I don't know how I'm going to raise her to be a proper Christian."

Lila shivered and waited to see what the woman would say next. Lila was quite familiar with that attitude. It ran in her family.

"The heathen." The woman rolled her eyes and clucked her tongue. "No wonder Alex left her. I have a mind to turn her over to the foster system."

"Well, it's a good thing that I'm Sera's power of attorney. That means I can decide where my great granddaughter goes. I can see it was a mistake to involve you."

"I'll take her," interjected Lila. She didn't know what came over her, but she couldn't let that woman damage Taela. The poor girl was already mourning the loss of her mother. She did not need to be thrown into a foster system. Lila bit the inside of her cheek and hoped she could talk Karter into going along with it.

"I'm not going to just hand her over to you." Gertrude's face reminded Lila of a scrunched up sour puss.

"Lila, please reach into the drawer there, will you? Pull out the manila envelope."

Lila did as Ginny asked. She pulled the envelope from the drawer and went to hand it to her, but the woman gestured for her to open it. Lila looked at the paperwork inside and found that Sera's mother had indeed declared her great grandmother to be in charge of the child. Had she known that the demon was coming for her? Reading further, she saw that Sera's last will and testament was included. It asked that her child be looked after by her distant cousin, Lila Dawson.

"Wait, what?" Lila was confused. "What does this mean?"

"I'll explain momentarily. But please tell her what it says."

"Sera asked for Taela to be left in my care, as one of her last living relatives."

"Can I see that?" Lila handed it over and saw the woman's face turn crimson. "I see it's been notarized."

"Yes. It's the real deal, Gertrude. Now, if you could be so kind as to hand the child over."

"She's all yours." Gertrude shoved the girl forward and sneered at them as she walked from the room.

Lila held her arms out to the girl and smiled as she flung herself into her arms. Tears were streaming down Taela's face. "Where is Keelo?"

"That horrible woman threw him away. I'm so sorry, Lila."

"Shhh. It's okay, sweetheart. We'll get you a new one. Not

to worry." How in the world was she going to explain this to Karter? Lila turned to Ginny. "I think your great grandmother has a story for me." Lila sat down in the chair next to Ginny and pulled Taela in her lap. "So...?"

"You were adopted."

"What?" So many things made sense with just that one admission. The way her siblings had treated her differently. How nothing Lila had done ever seemed to measure up to their satisfaction. She had always felt like an outsider, and now she knew why.

"Cecilia was your mother. She was a distant cousin on your mother's side of the family, with no real blood ties to her. Your mother had wanted another child, but had been unable to conceive again. When Cecilia made the decision to give you up for adoption, your mother talked your father into taking you into their family."

"Does this mean I am part of the Vinson bloodline?"

"Yes." Ginny smiled at her.

"And that's why he wants to kill me." Lila shivered.

"Yes. But that's also why you can destroy him. The same blood that conjured him can banish him."

"Banish who?" asked Taela.

"The thing that hurt your mother," Ginny answered her.

Lila raised her eyebrows at her, but Ginny waved off her concerns. "The child knows more than you think. It's better to tell her the truth, Lila."

"Is he going to hurt Lila?" Taela's face was filled with fear.

"No, darling. He's not. Lila is a fighter, and she won't rest until you are safe," Ginny predicted.

"I miss my mommy." Taela's lips wobbled.

"Oh, sweet girl. You'll see her again. I promise." Lila just had to banish the demon first, and then all of the spirits would be free again. Then Sera could look over her daughter from the other side, and if Taela was lucky, her mother would be able to speak to her.

Taela snuggled against her. "Can I really go home with you?"

"Yes, dear. But first, I have a few things I need to do. Would you mind spending some time with a friend of mine?" Lila knew exactly what she was going to do. "She has a little girl who would love to play with you."

"Really?" Her eyes lit up. Clearly, the child had not had much play time lately.

"Really." Lila turned to Ginny. "You're my grandmother, aren't you?"

"Yes. I am." Ginny's face lit up with a bright smile.

"Do me a favor?" Lila asked her.

"Yes?"

"Don't think about going anywhere, okay? I just met you."

"I'm not planning on it."

"Good. Well, wish me luck." Lila reached over and kissed her newfound grandmother on the cheek.

"Come back and see me soon?" The twinkling blue eyes were misting over slightly.

Lila realized that Ginny had lost a lot in the past month. She patted her on her hand and shook her head. "Of course."

"Where's my hug, sweet girl?" Ginny asked Taela

The little girl launched herself at her great grandmother. "I love you, Nana."

"Me too, darling. Me too. Be good for Lila, will you?"

"Yes, ma'am."

"We'll come back soon, I promise." Lila held her hand out to Taela. "Come love, you've got friends to make."

Chapter 21

Lila drove Taela to Brina's, hoping she had made the right decision. Letting her stay with that overbearing grandmother would have broken the child's spirit. Lila saw so much light in her, even among all the sorrow. She wanted to protect her from the bitterness in the world around them. A child should not have to deal with such loss. Lila hoped that Karter would understand her choices. If not, she would raise Taela by herself, even if it meant separating herself from the only man she would ever love.

"Taela, what has your grandmother told you about your mother?" Lila asked her curiously.

"That she was killed for being a witch. That it happens to all heathens," the child answered softly.

"That's not going to happen, Taela. I promise." Lila was filled with a mixture of emotions. Anger for the way that evil woman had treated this child, and a fierce need to protect her from the horrors that Lila was about to face.

"Will I be able to hear her again?" Taela asked her.

"I hope so, love. I really do." Lila bit her lip and wondered how she was going to explain all of this without it sounding as crazy as it was. Part of her wondered if her real mother was still alive. Should she look for her? Would that be too strange? What would she even say to her?

Lila shook her thoughts from her head. This was not the time to try to figure any of that out. She had a lot to do. If she didn't destroy that doll and break the connection Ezra had with this world, he would continue to rise to his power. Lila had a feeling that if he killed the entire line, he would finally materialize into this world. He had been draining the life of others to create enough power to roam this world like a mortal. That was how he was able to wrap his hands around her throat. She wasn't sure how this knowledge came to her, but she trusted it. The Vinson home and Witch's Hollow were both powerful vortexes. Lila had no idea what had created them or what magic possessed the doll, only that it was time to break those connections.

As she pulled into the driveway, she prayed that Brina would be able to take Taela. Just for a day or so, because Lila was afraid of what was going to happen next. When she parked the car, she turned around to smile at Taela. "Don't be afraid, love. You're going to love your Aunt Brina. She's going to be my sister soon. And Sophie is your cousin."

"I have a cousin?" Taela's face lit up.

"You sure do. Now, she's a little younger than you, so you're going to have to look after her, okay?"

"I promise." Taela held her hand up solemnly.

Lila got out of the car and helped Taela get out from her side. She reminded herself that they would need to get her a safety seat as soon as possible. "Let's go see if they're home, Taela." They walked up the steps and Lila smiled as Taela pushed the doorbell two times. "That's enough, Taela. I think I hear them."

The door opened and Brina greeted her with a smile. "Lila."

"I hope you don't mind. I have a favor to ask." Lila put her arm around Taela.

"Oh my goodness, who is this?" Brina smiled at the child.

"I'm Taela. Lila's going to be my mommy now. Are you my aunt now?" The child beamed up at Brina.

Brina's eyes shot to Lila's in surprise. "Well, welcome to the family, little miss. You can call me Aunt Brina. Your cousin is playing in the living room if you'd like to visit with her."

"Okay." Taela bolted into the doorway and disappeared from Lila's line of sight.

"I'm sorry. This just...well...."

"Does Karter know yet?" Brina asked her.

"This is a mess for sure. Can we talk?" Lila felt tears rising to the surface.

"Of course. Amber's inside, so we can sit outside if you like."

"That's a good idea."

"How is your ankle?" Brina asked her with concern.

"Good. I hardly feel any pain right now."

"You had us worried." Brina walked her to the bench in the garden.

"I know, and it's not over yet. There's so much to explain. I don't even know where to start."

"Start with Taela."

"I just found out that she's my cousin's child. That my entire life has been one lie after another. I went to visit Virginia Vinson. Turns out, I'm her granddaughter. My mother — well, my adopted mother wanted another child, so she adopted her cousin's child."

"Wow…that's a lot to take in. Are you all right?"

"That depends on how upset Karter's going to be. You see, Sera, Taela's mother, left her to me in her will. I'm not even sure how she knew." Lila sighed sadly.

"A witch's intuition is a powerful thing. And I don't think there's anything Karter could deny you. He loves you."

"Yes, I think he does. But is this too much for him?" She sniffled as she tried to keep the tears from falling.

"There's nothing he wouldn't do to make you happy. Besides, I kind of like the idea of watching him chase after a child."

"Yes, but it's sooner than if we had our own."

"Not much sooner, if you ask me." Brina's eyes twinkled knowingly.

Lila blushed. "It's too soon for that."

"If you say so." Brina teased Lila.

Lila fought the urge to put her hand on her stomach. Nothing would make her happier than to be carrying life inside her, but there was a dark cloud over her head. "I can't let myself think of that right now, Brina. I have to put an end to the demon that's haunting my family."

"How can I help?"

"Watch over Taela. Keep her safe. No matter what."

"What are you going to do, Lila?"

"Break its link from our world. I've got to get the doll that it's connected to. Ginny seems to think that it's channeling its energy from it. I tend to agree."

"That thing is hideous. I tried to tell Karter not to buy it, but he seemed to think it was the right thing to do. When it made its way to Virginia, she almost died. That's how she made her way to the homestead at her age."

"How did it get there?" Lila wondered aloud.

"No one really knows, but she knew what it was right away. Karter keeps it locked inside a glass cabinet at the club."

"I have to destroy it, Brina. The demon is getting closer to making his way to our world forever. If he gets his mortal form, there'll be no stopping him." Lila shuddered at the thought. While he only controlled spirits right now, very soon he would be taking over the living as well. She could not let that happen. Even if it meant...Lila could not allow herself to go down that road.

"What do you need from me, Lila?"

"If something were to happen to me, would you please take care of Taela? She's lost so much already. She needs to be in a stable home with people who will love her and raise her to not be afraid of who she is."

"It won't come to that." Brina put a hand on her to reassure her.

"But if it does—"

"Then she will be well protected." Brina's face took on a determined light. "You must know the power you hold inside you, Lila. I sensed it the moment we met."

"Me?" Lila almost squeaked.

"Yes, you. You are a powerful witch, Lila. Destined to do

great things."

Lila waved her words away. "I'm just one person, Brina."

"Don't go into the battle like that, Lila. You have to believe in yourself." Brina's words were more than a caution.

"I will take this thing down if it's the last thing I do, Brina. Rest assured he will not haunt any of my family ever again."

"Where do you think he originated, Lila?"

"I know he is tied to that house, but I don't think he started there. I have to bring the doll back to where it all started." Lila remembered the stone in the forest. She had a feeling that all the answers were deep under the ground there. Closing her eyes, she remembered the earthen crypt that she had to crawl her way out of in her dream. The demon had unknowingly given her the answer to his own destruction.

"You just figured something out."

"Yes." Lila folded her hands in her lap. "Stay out of the forest, Brina."

"I have no plans to go inside it any time soon." Brina put her hand over Lila's hand. "Goddess take you, Lila. You will be able to do what generations haven't been able to do."

Lila nodded at her. "I have no choice."

And she didn't. Lila knew that no matter the outcome, this was the only way to bring an end to the darkness that threatened the ones that she loved. She wasn't sure what would happen when she destroyed the doll, but she would face it with her head held high and over a century of witches surrounding her, many of which had called Witch's Hollow their home.

"I have to go see Karter now." Lila was not looking forward to it either. He was not going to be happy with the way their circumstances had changed.

"You should tell him everything," Brina recommended.

"I will," she lied. Lila could not tell him everything. If he knew what she was about to do, he would never let her go. She was afraid to let him go with her. Her dreams were a reflection of a possible future occurrence. If it meant he would die, then Lila could not let him get involved. If something happened to her, she knew Karter would take care of Taela. She imagined he would be reluctant to accept the child into their family, but over time he would grow to love her. That she was sure of. The outcome of what came next, that was the part she was still working out.

"Taela came with the clothes on her back, Brina. I haven't had a chance to get her anything."

"Don't you worry about a thing, dear girl. I love a good shopping trip."

"I've got some money in my purse."

"Nonsense. What fun is that? Let me spoil the child." Brina's face lit up with glee.

"You're going to make a good auntie," smiled Lila.

"And you're going to be an amazing mother."

Lila felt wistful for a moment. If her life worked out that way, Lila would be the luckiest woman in the world. "I have to go now, Brina. Thank you again."

"Of course."

As Lila walked away from Brina, she put a hand on her stomach and nibbled her bottom lip. She couldn't afford to let what could be stop her from taking care of the current problem. If she were pregnant, destroying this demon was the only thing that would guarantee her child's future.

Chapter 22

The drive to Glamz seemed to take an eternity. Her heart was pounding by the time she made it into the parking lot. What happened next could rewrite her entire future. She prayed that Karter would understand.

Making her way into the club, she was surprised to find there were a few customers milling about for lunch. She walked over to the bar and sat on a stool. Looking around her, she found the room covered with objects that had come from haunted houses around the world, none of which were giving off any kind of paranormal energy. Lila smirked. Of course not. Not every object was connected to the dead. Most of them seemed to hold only remnants of their pasts.

"What can I get you?" The female bartender asked her politely.

"Karter Knight."

"He's busy right now."

"He'll want to see me," Lila assured her.

"I doubt that," snickered another voice beside her.

"Shut up, Leonard." The woman narrowed her eyes on him.

Lila had a bad feeling about this. "Where is my fiancé?"

"Oh shit." The man looked away with a guilty look on his face.

"I didn't know he was engaged."

"Apparently, neither does he." The man's voice was hidden behind his hand.

Lila moved off her stool and held her head up high. Something was definitely going on, and neither one of these people were going to be any help to her. "Where's his office, please?"

The man held his hand up in front of him. "I got nothing."

"Ass." The girl snorted. "Up the stairs to the right, but I didn't tell you that."

"Of course not." Lila nodded to her and went in search of her mate.

When she made her way up the stairs, she could hear a woman's voice. Her heart sunk slightly as she pushed the door open. Lila closed the door quietly behind her and saw Karter sitting on a couch near the back of the room. The blonde she had seen the other day was on top of him, her hands pushing his shirt up as she kissed him on the lips.

"Oh, hell no!" Lila crossed her arms in front of her. "I don't know who the hell you think you are, but you will keep your skanky hands off my man!"

The woman turned around to face her, and Lila saw her for what she was. Her eyes were black holes, and large venomous fangs protruded from her mouth. Small black symbols were tattooed on her face, symbols that shifted and changed shape.

Her long fingers were covered with nails that were sharp enough to eviscerate her mate if Lila wasn't careful.

"It's not him you want, is it, succubus?" Lila's hands were now at her side with an electric current pulsing through them. The air crackled around her as her anger picked up.

"He'll do, though."

Her fingers sliced through the air toward Karter's neck. Before she could rip into him, a lightning bolt shot from Lila's hand. The succubus flew through the air and landed against the wall behind her. She dropped to her feet and launched herself at Lila. Lila cast a web of light around her and suspended her in the air.

"Now, you're going to tell me where he is."

"Go to hell," the woman spat at her.

"You first." Lila squeezed the light around the creature and her skin sizzled against it.

"You won't catch him. No one can."

"You have seriously underestimated me."

"And you have underestimated my control over your man."

Lila felt a pair of hands around her neck and tried to break the hold over her. She could not afford to lose sight of the succubus. Her mind called out to him. *Karter, please. You're hurting me.* The hands relaxed, but not enough for her to break free from him. *Karter. I love you.*

"Kill her!" a shrill scream erupted across the room, and Karter's hands started to squeeze harder.

Karter, if you kill me, you'll kill your child. While Lila had no confirmation, no physical proof, every inch of her believed her words. More than anything, she needed him to believe.

His hands dropped and a loud roar erupted from his mouth. She heard him change behind her, and when he was done, she felt his hot breath on her hands. He wanted to rip the succubus to shreds.

"Wait!" She warned him. Lila wasn't done with Julia. Not at all. She squeezed her fingers together and pulled the web of light closer.

The succubus shrieked. "I should have taken him out while I had the chance. Your love makes you too powerful."

"You're damn right it does. Never mess with a witch's wolf." So, it made a little more sense now. Ezra knew that together the two of them were unstoppable. While she wanted to face him alone, she knew that Karter would have to come with her if they were going to put an end to his evil. She would not rest until his wicked ways were obliterated from this world.

"You can't stop him," the blonde cackled.

Lila looked down at Keelan. "Finish her."

The wolf leapt at the succubus just as Lila released her hold over her. She turned her back so she didn't have to see what happened next. Snarling growls were interrupted by the crunch of bones as the wolf annihilated its foe. She heard a loud hiss and pop, and turned to find the succubus consumed in flames before it melted to a pile of ash. The wolf was dripping in blood. Lila felt the world shift before her as dizziness overtook her. She reached for a chair and sat down on it. Putting her head in her hands, she tried to make the dizzy feeling disappear. So much had happened so fast.

Two hands reached for her face, and Lila found herself looking into troubled blue eyes. "Lila...."

Sobs left her mouth as he crushed her against his body. "You could have died."

"I'm here. I'm fine. I'm more worried about you." His mouth kissed the top of her head. "I hurt you. Let me look at you." Lila looked away from him as he touched the fresh bruising around her neck. "Damn it."

"It wasn't your fault," she whispered.

"I almost—"

"You didn't." Lila grabbed his hands and pulled them away from her neck. "Where's the doll?"

"What?"

"The doll, Karter. We have to destroy it where it started."

"You're not even going to talk about what you said?"

Lila blushed. "I might have lied."

"Lila...." He grinned at her.

"Well...it worked. But we do need to talk about children."

"But you just said...."

Lila looked away from him. "I'm not who I thought I was."

"What do you mean, Lila?"

"I went to Rainier Homestead today to visit Virginia Vinson, only to find out that not only was I her missing grandchild, but also the appointed guardian to one small child."

"Which child?"

"Taela. It seems Sera knew her fate, and had her will made over a year ago. My bloodline is why that demon is haunting me. I have to destroy it, Karter. I don't have a choice."

"Okay. Let's do this."

"Do what exactly?"

"Destroy it."

"And what about Taela?"

"Your flesh and blood is mine too. I imagine she'll need a good family to keep her on the right path."

Lila launched herself into his arms and sighed against him. "Have I told you lately how much I love you?"

"Yes. I believe you have, but the feeling is mutual." Karter put his hand on her belly. "I also know when you're lying, Lila."

She shivered in his arms. "Do you really think it's true?"

"If it's not, it will be." His eyes flashed hot gold.

"You're covered in blood, Karter." She hadn't noticed it right away.

"Then help me wash it off." He nodded to the door behind him. "All the comforts of home."

"What if they hear us?"

"The room is sound proof. I like my privacy," he grinned.

"Karter Adam Knight, if you start telling me you bring all your women here, I just might have to castrate you." At least she knew why the people downstairs had not come running when the succubus screamed her head off. She wasn't sure they had time for this.

"Come with me, Lila." His eyes told her that she would be well rewarded if she did.

"There's no time, Karter. We have to get that doll to Witch's Hollow as soon as possible. The demon will not be happy that you destroyed its mate."

"I'll be quick," he promised her as his mouth came down on hers.

Lila felt her pulse jump at the base of her neck as Karter's hands ran under her shirt and strummed against her nipple. She had no idea how he could be so aroused at a moment like this, but found herself being led into the bathroom behind him. His desire started to light her own as his hands quickly undressed her. When he slid down her body to remove her pants, he kissed her belly, making her shiver against his lips.

"Karter...."

"You protest too much, Lila. Come. Let me love you." His mouth kissed her throat and she sighed against him. He stepped away from her, long enough to turn the shower on. When he tested the water to make sure it was warm enough, he crooked his finger at her. "I do believe you were about to thank me for saving your life."

"Saving *my* life?" Lila shook her head at him. "If I remember correctly, it was my magic that kept your ass alive."

"Says you. What are you afraid of, Lila?" He grinned at her as he took her hand in his. Turning it over, he kissed her palm softly before nibbling her wrist. Hot desire coiled in her belly, a desire she had been trying to keep at bay.

The adrenaline of moments before took over as he pulled her into his arms. As the hot water trickled over her, Lila sighed against him. She reached around to find a cloth to wash his face off. "Let me clean this off you."

Lila washed his face as quickly as she could, and when she was done she ran kisses all over it. "I thought I was going to lose you."

"I'm here, Lila." His mouth covered hers and she drew his tongue into her mouth. She tasted the warm water as it pooled over their faces. His fingers squeezed her ass and brought her closer to him.

"Someone is awfully worked up," Lila teased him when she felt his erection surging between them.

"Defending a mate has its advantages." He nibbled a path down her neck and pushed her breasts up with his hands so that he could draw them into his mouth one at a time. He backed her into the shower wall.

Lila moaned as he sucked her hard into his mouth. The intensity was growing stronger by the minute. She could sense the wild need inside him, and knew that if he continued her own would be just as bad. Lila lifted one of her legs and wrapped it around him. She drew him closer to her and felt his erection closer to her stomach.

Karter lifted her up against the wall and slid his cock inside her. Lila wrapped her legs around him and held onto him as he started to push into her. At first his movements were slow and deliberate, but Lila wanted more. "Please, Karter."

"Please what?" His voice was strained.

"Take me."

He growled and plunged deeper into her hot core. His movements became hard and fast as he let himself go. Lila's nails scratched hard against him, and her legs were like a vise around his waist as she held on for the ride. The faster he went, the more she wanted him. The steamy water around them only seemed to heighten the sensations.

"Yes, that's it. God, yes. Take it, Karter." She unraveled over him as she came hard against him. Karter slammed into her one last time before he joined her.

He unwrapped her legs and slid her down his body. "Next time, we'll go much slower, Lila."

"Says you. I had no problem with your performance." She

felt a haze of sexual slumber start to trickle through her body. Lila wished she could stay there in that moment forever with him, but there was still a lot that they needed to do. And while she wanted to take care of it herself, she was stronger with her mate by her side. Needing someone was not a weakness after all.

Karter turned off the water and helped her step out of the shower. He handed her a towel and she started to towel herself off. She turned to find Karter watching her every movement.

"You're really okay, Lila?" Concern filled his voice.

"Yes, I am, for the moment. But that could all change if we don't bring the doll to his lair." Lila shivered as she pulled her clothes back on.

"Then that's what we'll do. I should bring the pack with us."

"No, Karter. I need them protecting Ginny and Taela." Lila knew that if she left those two unguarded her plans could backfire. She didn't want that to happen.

"Fine. I'll get the doll." He walked over to the wall and moved a poster off the wall. Behind it was a large safe. Karter input the code and the door swung open. He quickly retrieved a large wooden box and closed the safe back up. "I didn't just put it out in the club, you know."

"I know. It was wrong of me to assume you would put the world at risk."

"They just needed the illusion that they were at risk."

"I understand. Let's not waste any time, though."

"Let's go."

Lila barely had time to stop and think. All that mattered

now was keeping the ones she loved safe. Their futures all depended on it.

Chapter 23

When they pulled into the driveway, Lila saw Taela looking out the window. Lila hadn't wanted to come here, but they had to explain to the others what needed to be done. As pack leader, Killian needed to know what was going on. Lila had very little experience with him, other than through the moments she had with Brina.

Killian came out of the front door and nodded to her. "Are you all right, Lila?"

"Sure, ask about her. I'm just chopped liver." Karter crossed his arms over his chest and gave his brother a disparaging glance.

"Oh, I'm sorry. Did you get a booboo?" Killian teased Karter.

"No," grumbled Karter. He glared at Killian.

"That's what I thought." Killian rolled his eyes.

"Boys...can we get down to the problem at hand?" Lila didn't think this was the time or place for a display of testosterone.

"So, you are planning on finding its lair, is that right?" Killian asked her.

"Yes. And I need the rest of you to keep my family safe."

"I don't like this—I don't like this at all." Killian shook his head.

"Please," whispered Lila. "I promise I won't let him die."

Killian's eyes rose in surprise. "Wow, she doesn't seem to like your odds."

Karter snorted. "I'll take my chances."

"I didn't mean...." Lila let out a frustrated breath. "Look, I'm stronger with him by my side. It's hard to explain. Besides, if he's with me, I won't be worried about him. I cannot afford to be distracted."

"I make her stronger." Karter held up his chin as if he were taller than his brother.

"Fine. Puff your chest out, but Brina will not let me hear the end of it if something happens to her. That kid's been through enough already." He nodded to the five-year-old who was watching Lila with a fearful expression.

"She knows." Lila sighed. "Excuse me, boys. I have to talk to her before we go."

Lila pushed past them and raced into the house. When she opened the door, Taela launched herself at her. "It's going to be okay, Taela."

"Please don't leave me." The child was shaking.

"Remember Grandma Tilly?" Lila asked her.

"Yes." The child nodded at her solemnly.

"She taught me never to run away from a fight. One day you'll understand that, Taela. I'm not afraid. I'm coming back to you, Taela."

193

"Promise?"

"I promise." At least that was her greatest hope. Whether she came out of this or not, she was taking that thing down with her.

Taela hugged her so tight, Lila was afraid the child would never let her go. Lila kissed the top of her head. "Take care of Sophie today, okay?"

"I will," promised Taela. The little girl pulled a necklace out of her pocket and held her hand up. "Take this, Lila."

"I gave that to you, little one."

"You have to take it." The girl's eyes were filled with fear for Lila's safety.

"Fine, but you are not to leave Aunt Brina's sight, do you understand?"

"Yes, ma'am," the girl promised solemnly.

"I'll be back, Taela." Lila ruffled her hair as she stepped away from her. She nodded to Brina, who was watching from the hallway. They did not need to exchange words at all. Brina would look after Taela no matter what. Lila was sure of it.

Lila sighed as she left the house. She saw Karter standing near the path leading into the woods, holding the small wooden box in his arms. As if he sensed her, he turned around. Lila memorized every detail. His blond hair seemed to shine in the sunlight. His handsome face was starting to grow stubble from not shaving for a few days. He wore a white T-shirt that showed off his muscled arms. His tight blue jeans made her wish they weren't heading off into the woods, but there was no hope for it. Sadness filled her thoughts for a brief moment, knowing this could be the last time she saw him on this earth. But Lila could not give in to those thoughts.

Lila took one step after another, her courage growing the closer she got to him. Her resolve could not be shaken, or all would be lost. She did not want to be responsible for the decimation of an entire family line.

Karter sensed the emotions racing through her. "It's going to be all right, Lila."

"It has to be." She gave him a reassuring smile.

"Stronger together," he reminded her. "No one messes with my witch."

"And no one touches my wolf," she returned. "Let's go, Karter."

As they traveled through the woods, Lila took in the area around her. The birds were vacant, a sign that Ezra had already made his path through the woods today. If he were here, then he couldn't be anywhere else, which was just a slight relief to her. She still had to worry about what was about to happen. Lila had not shared her dreams with Karter at all. He had no idea what he was walking into, and Lila did not have the energy to explain it right now. It was far easier to travel in silence.

When they made it to the stone where Lila had been attacked, she felt the demon's presence. He did not want them there, but he was not going to stop this. Lila put the necklace around her neck and said a silent prayer to the goddess above to protect her from the evil inside this place. Kneeling down, she touched the symbols on the rock and closed her eyes.

"Be careful, Lila," Karter cautioned her.

She nodded in response, but continued to let her instincts lead her. Tracing the symbols with her fingers, she sent her magic into the stone. The etchings started to glow bright white

195

as they heated up the rock below her. Large cracks appeared in the boulder and it split into hundreds of pieces which levitated in the air, showing the entrance to a large black hole in the ground.

"You ready, Karter?"

"Yes."

"I need him." Lila hated to ask him to transform, but the truth of the matter was that Karter was a lot more powerful in his wolf form. If he were injured as a wolf, he would heal much faster than if he were injured in his mortal form.

Lila took the box from him and waited for him to transform. She watched his body shrink into itself, something that looked incredibly painful. It was hard to watch, but Lila needed to see how much it took to be the man he was every day. His life was a gift and a curse, for with great power came immense pain. She held out her hand and stroked Keelan's head. Lowering herself to the ground, she nuzzled her nose against the wolf's. "I love you, forever and always."

His eyes closed as he nuzzled her neck with his nose. She wrapped her arms around the wolf's neck and summoned the courage to lead them into the darkness. Sliding into the hole in front of her, she felt something reach for her, and before she could stop it, she found herself separated from Karter. "Karter!" she screamed.

The wolf tried to enter the hole, but the ground shook around her, and a slide of dirt and debris closed over the hole. His angry growls and howls could be heard on the other side. Lila drew her knees up to her chest as she tried to figure out how much trouble she was in. She used her magic to create a gentle glow of light around her. Lila was in a tunnel that was barely tall enough for her to crawl through.

"Well, that's fantastic."

Lila?

I'm here, Karter. I'm okay.

I'm getting help.

Don't go, Karter. Lila was afraid if he left the area her ability to keep him safe would disappear. He never answered her, and while worried something had happened to him, she realized he was just refusing to do what she asked. Lila shivered as something crept past her foot. She could not allow her imagination to run away with her. Just because she had dreamt about reanimated body parts did not mean that would actually happen here.

"Get it together, Lila." She pushed the box ahead of her as she crawled on her belly. Lila had no idea how far she was going to have to travel, only that she would find the answers at the end of the tunnel.

The further she moved, the more space opened up before her, until the tunnel finally opened up into a large dirt cavern. She opened her hand and created a ball of light that lit the area up around her. She saw a pedestal with candles. Flicking her hand, she tossed the flame at the wick and breathed a sigh of relief when light cast itself around the room. She did the same for the other candles that circled the room.

When the light absorbed the darkness around her, her eyes caught upon a skeleton that was nailed to a pillar at the back of the earthen room. While most skeletons degraded over time, this one seemed to be regenerating, and Lila realized that this was the mortal that Ezra must have taken over in this world. His spirit was not entangled in the body at the moment, but that could change in moments if she weren't lucky.

Lila opened the box and looked at the doll for the first time. It was a ceramic baby doll, with small cracks that seemed to be ingrained into the skin like dull veins beneath the surface of skin. The body was covered in an old christening gown that was wrinkled and faded by the passage of time.

When Lila went to touch the head, it rotated in her hands. The eyes snapped open to reveal a dark black void. A screech left its mouth as a darkness filtered from it. Lila threw the doll down on the ground and stomped on its head with all her might. The force of her foot on its face had no effect whatsoever. She raised her hand and a magic wind rose around her, as she called for help from the witches long past. "Take this soul back to the other world, cast him out from the light and send him back to darkest night where he belongs."

Red symbols rotated around her as her ancestors and all the lost souls he fed on brought their light into the fight. She raised her hand and sent them hurtling into the doll. Red cracks formed inside the ceramics, as the light started to dissolve the doll one inch at a time. It looked like the doll was being incinerated by hot molten lava. A loud shrill filled the air, and Lila fought the urge to cover her ears. Standing her ground, she felt a wild magic racing through her as her soul was reinforced. Lila felt the pentacle around her neck glowing, and she smiled. Amber Knight must be sending her help from the other side of this tunnel. She would have to thank her later.

Just as the doll exploded before her, the darkness slithered from it like a deathly coil and it launched itself toward the skeleton. Lila had expected as much, and while she wanted to cut it off at the pass, she knew to destroy its hold over this land, she had to let the powers merge to destroy them once and for all.

Drawing herself up to her full height, Lila prepared herself for the next part of the battle. A dark oily light circled around the skeleton, entangling itself into the structure of bones. She watched as the muscles filled in around the network of flesh that was molding over it.

"Are you ready to meet your maker, witch?" The jaws of the skeleton moved in a way no dead person should.

Lila fought the shiver running up her spine. "You first."

Ezra cackled at her. "Once I take you down, the child is next."

Lila's anger grew. "You're not going to hurt anyone ever again."

"Who's going to stop me? You?"

"We are," a voice growled as it leapt into the tunnel. Karter's human form jumped into the air and shifted mid-flight before tackling the creature.

Lila felt panic rise as the demon shook him off so hard that he slammed into the wall with a loud whimper.

"No one hurts my man!"

Lightning shot from her fingertips and electrified the demon in front of her. She heard a sizzle as its flesh started to catch fire before her. Ezra charged at her and knocked her to the ground. She felt his hands squeeze her throat, and knew that this had been his endgame all along. Lila had other plans though. Reaching her hands up to her neck, she sent all her raging wrath into the demon's body. The skeleton started to sizzle and shake as he held onto her. He tried to pull away from her, but she refused to release him. As his hands squeezed harder, she struggled to breathe. As his life faded before her eyes, she started to lose conscious.

Keelan launched through the air, his snarls only interrupted by the sound of flesh being torn from bone. Lila choked out a few words as the demon was fading from this life. "I banish thee, Ezra, to your eternal sleep on the other side. I bind you from doing harm to another life. So mote it be!"

An explosion of flame erupted before them and the cave was filled with a raging inferno. Smoke filled her already struggling lungs, and Lila tried to fight the dizzy waves that were dragging her under. She looked around for Karter, but did not see him anywhere. As the darkness overwhelmed her, Lila's last thoughts were for the future she prayed still existed.

Lila heard a voice near her ear. "Don't you dare think about leaving me, Lila." He called out to his brothers. "Help me get her out of here."

Lila choked on the smoke, but she refused to give in. She rolled over on her stomach and started to crawl toward the tunnel that had led her in.

"That's right, Lila. Keep moving." Karter moved in front of her so that his face was next to hers. He crawled backwards, helping pull her out as he did. "Don't give up now, Lila."

Lila saw the terror he was trying to keep hidden from his face. She knew he was afraid of losing her, but Lila wasn't about to give up now. She would fight like hell to get out of this no matter what it took. Closing her eyes, she let herself think of all the things that were waiting for her on the other side.

As he pulled her out of the tunnel, a large flame erupted from the entrance. The ground shook and the dirt behind them collapsed inward.

Karter pulled her into his arms and cradled her close. "If you ever do that again, I just might have to kill you myself."

She coughed and sputtered in an attempt to get some words out. Instead, she stroked his face with her hand. Lila had no plans to attack any demons in the near future. She had done everything she set out to do. Her eyes met his. *I love you, Karter.*

"Damn right you do." He grinned at her and kissed her on the forehead.

"Everything all right?" Killian asked him.

"Thanks for pulling us out." Karter looked over to his brother and his eyes were filled with tears.

"It's what we do, brother." Killian patted him on the back. "So, are we all good?"

Lila nodded at Killan and gestured to her throat. Then she looked at Karter. *Tell him the demon is gone. We're safe.*

Karter gave his brother a cheeky grin. "She wants to know if you can watch Taela for the rest of the week. Apparently, slaying demons makes her —"

Lila glared at Karter and gave him a warning with her fist. *Karter Adam Knight!*

"Oooh, I know that look. Did she use the middle name?"

"Damn skippy," Karter grinned.

Lila shook her head as the two brothers erupted in laughing fits. How they could be laughing at a time like this, she had no idea. She sighed in defeat as they continued to tease each other. Lila rubbed her forehead in aggravation. *Can we go home now?*

Karter stopped laughing. "As soon as we make sure you're okay."

No doctors. Lila crossed her arms over her chest. She didn't want to explain what had happened to her. A normal doctor would assume that Karter had wrapped his hands around her throat.

"Fine. We'll go to Knight's Orchard."

"Good idea. Mother's probably fit to be tied anyway."

Killian helped Karter to his feet. The two of them helped Lila up and helped her walk away from the destruction behind her.

Chapter 24

As the months passed, Lila had seen her world change in ways she never dreamed of. With life restored around her, she had so many things to be thankful for. Today would be a day that she hoped they would remember for the rest of their lives.

She looked down at the little girl at her side and smiled. Taela was wearing a beautiful white dress with a blue satin sash around the middle that was tied in a large bow in the back. Lila had taken great care to style her hair like a princess. Today was all about her, after all.

As they walked into the courtroom, Karter leaned over and kissed Taela on the forehead. "You ready, munchkin?"

"Yes," came Taela's nervous response. "What if they say no?"

"Don't worry, love. They won't say no," promised Lila.

As they approached the attorney at the front of the court, Lila felt a twinge of something deep inside her and smiled secretly. There were a few surprises around the corner for all of them, but first things first.

"The judge is ready to begin." Margaret Meane gestured for them to join her.

"We're here today to see to the formal adoption of Miss Taela Renee Lewis-Vinson by Lila and Karter Knight. Are there any objections to the proceedings?"

"No, Your Honor." Virginia Vinson's eyes twinkled in delight as she answered the question. "My granddaughter's wishes were clear."

"I see. Do you agree to take on the responsibility of this minor?" The judge asked them.

"Yes," Karter answered with a nod of his head. He smiled down at Taela and patted her shoulder comfortingly.

"And you, Mrs. Knight?" The judge asked her.

"Absolutely." Lila glanced down at Taela as the child beamed up at her.

"Then I see no reason why we can't make it official." The judge rifled through his papers and his eyebrows rose curiously. "And you, Miss Taela, do you promise to take care of your siblings and treat them as if they were your own? Twins, is it?"

Lila smiled at the judge as two voices erupted at the same time.

"What?" Karter was looking at his wife in surprise.

"I knew it!" Amber Knight wrinkled her nose at her family. "You can pay me later."

Taela cleared her throat. "Eh hem. Sir, I promise to be the best big sister ever."

"Then I declare this adoption final, and from here on out the minor shall be known as Taela Renee Knight.

Congratulations to you and yours."

Lila mouthed her thanks to the judge, who gave her a big smile. She could not look at Karter right now, for tears were already filling her eyes. His hand touched her cheek and she turned to face him.

"You realize we're going to need a bigger house, right?" Karter kissed her on the forehead.

"It would appear so." Lila smiled at him. "Good thing we know someone who will cut us a deal."

"Killian's been wanting to get his hands dirty for a while now. You know how antsy he's been with this baby."

"That's only because I'm going to be henpecked," Killian interjected from behind them.

"Serves you right," Karter teased him.

"Hey, watch what you're saying. She's got two of them inside her, and you already have one. You're about to be in the same boat, brother."

Karter looked panicked for a moment. "When can we find out what we're having?"

"I thought I'd keep it a surprise." Lila giggled at the pained expression on his face.

"Like hell!" he grumbled.

Taela put her head against Lila's stomach. "Can I name my brothers?"

Everyone looked at Taela and Amber commented, "You all heard that. I'll be collecting my money at the end of the day, so make sure you ante up."

The courtroom was filled with laughter as the family rejoiced over the happiness that surrounded them. The dark clouds had faded, and now the only thing left to do was to live her life to the fullest. Lila planned to do just that.

About the Author

Ever since childhood, Elissa Daye has enjoyed reading stories as an escape from life. When she was a teenager she started to write her own stories that kept her entertained when she ran out of books to read. When she was accepted into Illinois Summer School for the Arts in her Junior year of High School, she knew she wanted to become a writer. Elissa graduated from Illinois State University in December 1999 with a Bachelor of Science in Elementary Education and began her teaching career, hoping to find moments to write in her free time.

After seven years of teaching, Elissa decided to focus on her writing and made the decision to put her teaching years behind her so that she could create the stories she had always dreamed of. She is now happily married and a stay at home mom, who writes in every spare moment she can find, doing her best to master the art of multitasking to get everything accomplished.